REBECCA AND JADE

CHOICES

REBECCA AND JADE

CHOICES

ELEANOR WATKINS

DERNIER PUBLISHING

London

Text copyright © Eleanor Watkins 2017
Cover illustration copyright © Rebecca Teall 2017
This edition copyright © Dernier Publishing 2017

Published by Dernier Publishing
P.O. Box 793, Orpington, BR6 1FA, England
www.dernierpublishing.com

ISBN 978 0 9569043 93

Typeset by Pete Barnsley (CreativeHoot)

REBECCA *AND* JADE

CHOICES

Contents

Part Two – A New Start

PART ONE

The Beginning

One

The Clinic

REBECCA

It wasn't the place I'd have chosen to be, on a breezy February morning. Through the window a pale winter sun was shining and I could see a drift of snowdrops under a nearby tree. I looked around the room. Vibrant yellow walls, which I guess were painted that colour to bring a cheery feel. Bright flower pictures, of poppies and sunflowers and marigolds, probably chosen for the same reason. I couldn't help feeling that something a bit more soothing, perhaps calm pastel blues or greens, would have been a better choice.

I kept fidgeting on the fake leather bench seat, which squeaked embarrassingly every time I moved. A pile of magazines – quite recent ones, not the usual three-year-old copies you get in most waiting rooms – sat in a neat pile on a little table. They were wasted on me though: I couldn't have concentrated on a magazine at that moment to save my life.

All this cheery stuff was not working at all. I glanced around the room again. Not one person looked happy to be there. The dark-haired girl opposite me caught my eye, and I tried to smile in a friendly way, but the smile died on my lips as she just gave me a steely stare and then looked away. She looked about my age, wearing skinny jeans and a pair of silver trainers I'd have died for. The blonde girl in the corner had shrunk into the smallest possible space as though she'd like to hide away, and was hunched up with her chin in her hands. Someone was talking to her – maybe it was her mother; maybe even a social worker – but I couldn't hear what she said. The girl didn't reply; she just shrugged her shoulders and let her hair fall forward to cover her face.

Two or three others, then there was Jade, sharing my blue plastic bench seat, looking as cool as usual, flicking through a fashion magazine, immaculate and relaxed, with long slim crossed legs and one turquoise ballet slipper dangling casually from her coffee-coloured toes with their perfectly polished nails.

I shifted in my seat, which squeaked again, and nibbled nervously at my nails. Someone came out of the consulting room and another name came up on the board. I wondered how much longer before our turn.

Jade was eyeing me critically over the page of her magazine. "Stop chewing your nails, Rebecca. It doesn't do anything for your image, you know." I was thankful she'd spoken in a low tone and the others hadn't heard. At least she'd never publicly humiliate me. And after this, I felt we would be friends for life.

"Are you sure they'll let us go in together?" I asked, not for the first time.

"Course they will. You can always take someone along to a consultation."

"Yes, but it's usually a relative, isn't it?"

"Doesn't have to be. Especially if you don't have any, or don't want them with you. Relatives, I mean. Don't worry. It'll be OK. Relax. Take a chill pill."

She flicked over a page and studied an article called *Dress to Impress*. Jade's future was all planned out. She'd spent a long time on YouTube studying how millionaires had made it big and had devised a life plan of her own. Good exam grades, then business college, making the right contacts, rising swiftly to the top of the tree, making pots of money and having it all, successful career, big house, swimming pool, fast cars, exotic holidays. I had no doubts she could do it, too. She's a bright girl and knew the score. She thought I was a complete wimp because I wanted to be a writer.

"Well, I suppose that's OK if you get to be a bestseller, like that woman who wrote *Fifty Shades of*

Grey," she said when I first told her of my ambitions. She'd looked at me dubiously. "But do you think you're good enough for that?"

I shook my head. "I don't want to write that kind of stuff."

"It's what makes the money."

"I don't care about the money. I just want to write about, well, the world and the things in it, and people, and their thoughts and feelings. Maybe I'll write poetry . . ." I stopped, because she was looking at me as though I'd completely lost it.

"You're a bit of a fruitcake, Becs, you know that? You need to get out more. Get a real life."

Well, maybe I was a bit of a dreamer and needed a dose of reality. I certainly didn't expect to find it in a place like this, though.

Another patient had emerged and another name came up on the board. Still not our turn. I wondered what exactly went on in there. All this waiting was setting my nerves on edge.

To take my mind off it, I thought about what would be happening in school right now. We'd be missing English, which was my fave subject. I'd been enjoying sixth form, enjoying the feeling of being more in control, not so much like a kid any more. We had our own common room and somewhere to make tea and coffee. A couple of the girls were taking their driving tests soon. One of the boys actually had his licence, and drove to school in his own car. It was only an old Fiat handed down from his older brother, but how cool must it be to have your own set of wheels?

The blonde girl had gone in, accompanied by the older woman, who almost had to push her along in front of her. As she passed I could see the girl's face, white and frightened and tense, as though she was having to make a huge effort to hold it all together.

I was amazed at how young she looked. Thirteen or fourteen, at a guess, two or three years younger than Jade and me. Surely she couldn't be pregnant? Yet why else would she be here, in this clinic? I sighed, and began to bite my nails again, but Jade's eye was on me and I twiddled my hair instead. She heaved a sigh herself, rolled her eyes and went back to her magazine, giving me up as a hopeless case. Nothing seemed to faze her. Not even when, after another long wait sitting in silence, the next name came up on the board and it was our turn to go in.

Two

Making an Impression

JADE

I was a bit late for the new school that first day, but that didn't bother me. I have never been one to stress too much about other people's expectations.

Susan and Paul made quite a fuss that first morning, making sure I had everything and preparing a big breakfast. I wish I could say they'd kept it up, but it soon became a case of grab your own. Susan offered to come to the school with me, can you believe it, or even come in and have a word with my class teacher.

"Whatever for?" I asked, spreading marmalade on my toast. "I'm sixteen, for goodness sake, starting A-levels, not a five-year-old starting school."

"Just trying to help," said Susan. "First day and all that. Zack, keep your sticky fingers off Jade's new bag."

9

This was to one of the eight-year-old twins she and Paul were also fostering. I was definitely getting preferential treatment at the moment, possibly because foster parents get enhanced payments for problem teenagers.

"I can hack it," I said, and took a bite of the toast. "Can I have another cup of tea?"

She got the teapot.

I had to admit I quite liked the school uniform. In a way it was disappointing that there was a uniform; if I'd stayed at my old school I could have worn a suit. Still, this was way better than some of the uniforms I'd had when I was younger. Some had been totally unflattering, and one school even had hats – kind of boater things with little ribbons. I ask you! Thankfully this one had the option of skirts as well as trousers. School trousers are the pits: plain and boring, neither skinny nor grungy. At least with a skirt you can wear it nice and short, and black tights show off your legs, which is cool. And you can also undo an extra button or two on the shirt, if you have a nice cleavage line. Good to know how to use your assets.

I spent a while trying to decide how to wear my hair. Up or down? Plait or ponytail? In the end, I did it up in a simple twist; less is more sometimes. I didn't hold back on the make-up though, not that I knew whether it was allowed or not. If anyone said anything, I could say it was allowed at my last school. Not true, but who was going to bother checking? And I added my gold hoop earrings.

On the way there I managed to take a wrong turning, which was why I was a bit late. No big deal. Once in the school I found the classroom easily enough, full of chattering Year Twelves, but a hush fell when I walked in. Well, no bad thing, first impressions are always important.

I soon had people sussed out. I'm good at that. The class teacher, for a start. A youngish man, not bad looking. He wouldn't be a problem. The lads were, well, lads, the same as anywhere. Acting a bit tough, pretending to be big men, most of them, and checking out the girls while pretending not to. One or two of the girls stood out. There was one who had long dark hair and blue-grey eyes, who I heard someone call Siobhan, so guessed she had Irish family. And a platinum blonde, Suzie, whose hair colour you could tell had never seen the inside of a bottle.

I hardly noticed Rebecca at all to begin with. She seemed to be one of those quiet, shy people who allow other people to walk all over them. I thought she looked very ordinary, until at some point she caught my eye and smiled – the kind of smile that lit up her whole face and somehow made you feel that you really mattered. Which was strange, seeing as we'd never set eyes on each other before that morning and hadn't even spoken. I managed to smile in return but then quickly turned away.

At lunch time, the class teacher, Mr Phelps, who also taught maths, came over and spoke to me. "Settling in OK, Jade? Need any help?"

I flashed him a dazzling smile, and turned on the full charm. "I'm fine, thank you, Mr Phelps."

"Well – er – if you need anything, just ask." He looked like he was floundering a bit and looked round for inspiration. "I'm sure Rebecca will help, if need be." He beckoned Rebecca over and said, "Just help Jade settle in, will you, Rebecca?" He went off looking relieved, as though he'd escaped the jaws of a man-eating tiger or something. I had to smile inside. Exactly the reaction I was hoping for. If I needed anything, he would get it for me.

Rebecca came over and said hello, though she was quite shy about it. She had nice hair, brown and shiny, and hazel eyes. I was polite but kept a bit of distance. I hadn't had a real friend for years, and saw no point in getting too pally with anyone until I had things properly sized up. She tried a bit of small talk and then went back to her mates. They hadn't come over with her, and were giving me wary looks. They were both attractive girls, Suzie, the platinum blonde, and Kelly, small and pretty. I suppose they thought I posed a threat to them, as I often seemed to do with girls my age. Well, they needn't worry. I wasn't at all interested in any of their male classmates, and wasn't likely to be. If the right man came along and fitted in with my plans, great. Until then, I'd rather not have the bother of relationships, especially with spotty sixteen-year-olds.

I kept my eyes and ears open for the rest of the day. By the end of it, I'd pretty much sussed out most of the people in the class. Ordinary, average, most of them, with few exceptions. The quiet ones, the loud ones, the geeky ones, the show-offs like Suzie, who kept flicking her hair about so that nobody could fail to see how blonde she was. Someone should tell her that a little more subtlety might be cool. The Irish girl, Siobhan, had a short fuse and could throw a fit very quickly, but the others respected her for it. A girl called Priya, one of the geeky ones, wore glasses and sometimes was referred to as Four Eyes, especially by the lads with big mouths. Creeps. Although I did wonder why nobody had advised her to try contact lenses.

Rebecca was the one who interested me the most, because of her amazing smile, which seemed to light up the whole room. I wondered what it would be like to have a real friend again. I was wary, but Rebecca's smile drew me like a magnet, somehow. I'd done pretty well without friends in the last year or two, focusing on my life plan. My assets – my looks and brains and street-wise savvy – were going to take me far away from this dull life into a world of luxury where I'd have everything I wanted, whenever I wanted it. I was going to make a success of my life. Despite frequent upheavals and changes of home, I was well on track. All my GCSEs were As and A*s, thanks to my own hard work; A-levels was next on the list.

That other little part of myself I could easily squeeze away in a corner and ignore, no problems. I'd been doing it long enough.

Three

Belonging

JADE

I didn't think of my mother at all any more. Well, not very often. Now and again, whether I wanted to or not, a memory would flash into my mind of this fair-haired, round-faced, soft-skinned person, who hugged me close and blew raspberries into my tummy and made me laugh. I once had a photo of my mum and me which fitted in with this, but it had got lost long before, on one of my many moves. I missed it for a while, but, hey, that was in the past and you had to get on with things.

I had a laugh to myself when I thought of the story I used to make up (and sometimes told other kids), that my mother was working as a model in the States, and that soon she'd come back and fetch me and we'd live in this massive house with a swimming pool and its own movie theatre. I've learned since then that if you want those things, you have to be the one to get them for yourself.

The reality of my early life was very different. I'd been told that my mother died when I was three, and I was passed round various relatives to begin with. My Jamaican father was long gone well before I was born.

I had grandparents (my mum's parents), but they'd fallen out with my mother over her relationship with my dad, and had nothing to do with us, so I've been told. They did take me in for a while, but it didn't last long. I was a difficult child, apparently. One or two other relatives tried having me for a while, although I don't really remember much. I'm told I screamed and kicked a lot. Only when Social Services were called in did they find the reason for my screaming; an untreated ear infection that led to a perforated eardrum. I don't remember any of it, but a nurse told me I must have been in agonising pain.

Anyway, my grandparents washed their hands of me and moved to Spain, and from then on it had been foster homes all the way.

I liked the first home I landed in; it was like being part of a real family. I had a mum and a dad, a sister who was a year older than me, and a little brother. My sister and I had identical dolls at Christmas and we sometimes wore matching outfits. We had a trampoline in the garden, went on trips to the seaside, and had a tabby cat called Marty. I stayed with them for two years and started school while I was there.

I thought I would be with them forever, but something happened. I didn't understand it at the time, though I must have been told, but I guess it must have been to do with the dad's work. The family moved to the other end of the country. They took my brother, my sister, and Marty. Me, they left behind. Because they all belonged, and I didn't.

I remember crying and pleading with them to take me, and the mum crying too, and my sister giving me a last hug, but a lady from Social Services was there and she took me very firmly by the hand and bundled me into her car. I bit her hand when she was buckling me into the car seat, and kicked the back of her seat all through the journey, until she handed me over to another lady, with the remark, "You'll have your hands full with this one."

Some things you don't forget. I think I made up my mind, then and there, that I wasn't going to get close to anyone again. I've lost count of the number of homes I've been in since then, some of them not for long. After that first family I began to fantasise about my real mum, and held on to the hope that one day she'd come back for me. One day, though, my case worker, Jenny, visited my school and heard me boasting to another girl. She took me to the head teacher's room.

"Jade, there are some things you ought to know." I looked at her. She was OK as social workers go – she kept her cool and didn't get on her high horse with difficult kids. She had a small furrow on her brow and I sensed I wouldn't like what was to come.

"What things?"

"About your mother. She won't be coming back, you know. She can't. I'm afraid she died, a long time ago."

I must have been told this before, but I clenched my fists and curled my toes in denial. "You're lying!"

"No, Jade. It's the truth. She died when you were three."

"She didn't."

Jenny sighed. "My dear, you have to accept it. I know it's hard. Would you like a hug?"

"No." I was furious, and wanted to kick her for destroying my fantasy. But I knew, deep down, that it was true, and the last bit of hope I'd had of belonging to a real family had died. It was several years later I discovered that my young mother, overwhelmed by the struggle of being a single parent, had taken to drugs and accidentally overdosed.

So I got used to moving. The last couple I'd been with were retiring from fostering. Bill had health issues, apparently, and wanted to get rid of me as soon as possible.

"Normally," said Jasmine, my latest social worker, "retiring parents would be expected to wait until their current child or children was leaving foster care, to cause the least disruption possible. They're willing to keep you on until, say, the end of term, but ideally, it would be sooner rather than later. What do you think?"

I shrugged. I'd been moved so many times that it didn't bother me really. I hadn't noticed Bill had health issues, but if they wanted me gone, fair enough. It made me laugh how social workers asked my opinion, though. More than once I worked that to my advantage. One time I'd been sharing a room with another girl and wanted my own space, so I mentioned this to the social worker and added, kind of sarkily, "A place with a swimming pool would be nice." I couldn't believe it when they moved me to a big house with a massive room all to myself, and yes, a swimming pool in the garden! I messed up there though. After an argument with another girl, I threw a takeaway curry and chips into the pool, and they had to get it drained and cleaned. I didn't stay there very long.

There were other episodes, too, at other places. Once when I was about thirteen I had a blazing row with one of the foster mums, ran off and hid in a shed at the bottom of the garden. Nobody knew I was there, so I stayed for a couple of days, sneaking out when it was dark to scrounge food from the back of a burger joint, where I knew one of the lads who worked there. I might have held out longer if the police hadn't got involved and one of them nabbed me coming out of the public toilets.

Anyway, when Jasmine asked, "Would you mind very much if your next home was in another area, with a new school, maybe under a new local authority?" I thought, yeah, why not. Might be a change for the better. Bring it on. I'd made my life plan by then, and a new start might be just what I needed.

So here I was, new town, new school, new foster home. Susan was youngish and a bit inclined to flap. The only time she really chilled was when she put her feet up and played pointless games on her tablet, or was chatting to her mates on social media. It helped if she could have a fag too, but in fairness to her she usually went outside for that. Paul smoked too, mostly out in the back garden or in his shed, where he escaped now and then to get away from the kids. I'd have liked to be the only child, but there were twin boys there, Zack and Ty, mixed race like me. Jasmine thought I'd fit in with the family, and that other children might be good for me. I didn't care that much one way or the other, as long as I could study in peace.

"We want you to be happy here," Susan said when I first went to look round. I sniffed a bit – the house was much like anywhere else on an old housing estate, a bit rough and showing signs of hard use from kids. Not a patch on the place with the swimming pool, but with any luck I would be off to uni in under two years, if everything went according to plan.

So I smiled and said, "I'm sure this will be fine," in my sweetest voice. Susan looked pleased but Jasmine had a kind of quizzical look. She knew me better. No doubt she and Susan would be having a private little chat over a cup of tea when I was well out of the way.

Four

A New Friendship

REBECCA

It was in Year Twelve that Jade started coming to our school. I remember it was the start of the autumn term, because we were all trying to settle down in the sixth form, with new teachers, and our class tutor was Mr Phelps. Most of us girls were in a twitter, catching up with what we'd done over the summer, where we'd been for hols and so on. My mates Suzie and Kelly had both been on sunshine holidays abroad, lucky them, while I'd only been to Devon. But the sun had shone that week, so we all had nice tans, which we were comparing, along with our new haircuts. There was also a bit of a buzz among the girls because Mr Phelps was young, not bad looking and quite fit with it. The boys as usual were eyeing us up and making a few comments. I noticed Adam, but made a point of pretending not to.

There was a hush when the new girl came in, especially as she was late. I guarantee there was not one person in the room who didn't notice her. You couldn't help it really, because she could only be described as drop-dead gorgeous. She surveyed us all coolly.

"Sorry I'm late. Where do I sit?"

The others came to life again. Mr Phelps, whose mouth I could swear had dropped open a little, recovered himself and said, "You must be Jade Thompson? You can take this seat."

She sashayed across the room and dumped her bag beside the chair. Thirty pairs of eyes followed her. You couldn't blame them really. She had to be the most exquisite person we'd ever seen in school. Dark skin, thick curly hair, long and shiny and done up in a twist. Chiselled features, huge dark eyes with long lashes and a figure to die for. I sneaked a glance at Adam and he was looking with the rest.

My heart sank. I'd never stand a chance with this new girl about, and I really liked him, more than I'd ever liked any boy before. He looked a bit like a picture I've seen of a young poet called Byron, dark-eyed and brooding, with longish curly hair and a thoughtful expression. Not like most of the others, who liked to act macho and tried to impress. He'd been in my English lit class last year, and we'd spoken once or twice, mostly about books, nothing much, but enough to make me feel we might have things in common. And here he was, practically drooling over Jade, like all the rest.

Still, she didn't appear to be interested in him, or anyone else, actually. She sat on her own, and I felt it must be a bit lonely for her, not knowing anyone here. I made up my mind there and then that I'd be friendly.

It must have been just a week or two into term that us sixth formers were roped in to helping with the set for the school orchestra's production of Peter and the Wolf. Most of us enjoyed the change whenever we had a free period. The art teacher, Mrs Walters, put us into pairs to paint a piece of scenery for the background. I'm not sure how I ended up with Jade, but I did, mixing shades of green on to canvas to represent a pine forest. Even then, with a blob of hunting-green poster paint on one cheek and hair scrunched back in an elastic band, Jade managed to look like a million dollars.

All the boys had been angling to partner with her, and even now they were edging as near as they could with their own part of the project. She gave them a scornful look. "Creeps," she said, and turned her back. I noticed it didn't stop her doing a little hip sway as she moved away, though, to keep them interested. It gave me a sick kind of feeling to see that Adam was in the nearest group. I couldn't help saying a word in his defence, though.

"Some of them are OK," I murmured.

She turned and gave me a look with her penetrating

dark eyes, green paint dripping from her brush. "Any particular one?"

I shook my head, but I could feel a tell-tale blush creeping over my cheeks. She laughed and slapped some paint on the canvas. "There is someone, isn't there? Now, let me guess. It wouldn't be that curly-haired one, would it? Adam?"

"Keep your voice down!" I pleaded, and she laughed again.

"OK, your secret's safe with me."

"There isn't any secret."

"If you say so. But here's some advice from your Auntie Jade. Always be the one who calls the shots. Treat 'em mean and keep 'em keen. They'll soon be eating out of your hand."

All very well for you, I thought, dipping my own brush into the paint. You've got it all, in spades, looks, figure, clothes sense, confidence. Not like shy, nervous me, with an average face and average figure and nothing much else to recommend me. I doubted if I'd ever get a half-decent boyfriend, let alone Adam, who'd probably forgotten he and I ever had a conversation.

All the same, there was something about Jade that I liked. She had a kind of resilience, a determination that nothing would get the better of her, a courage in the face of difficulty. And things hadn't been easy for her. She lived in a foster home. I was quite shocked when she told me that, imagining a kind of institution with a lot of problem kids. But she invited me back with her one day and it wasn't like that at all. She lived with a youngish couple on a housing estate, and two other little boys.

She had her own room though, and kept it neat, in contrast to the rest of the house, which seemed casual to say the least. Piles of stuff everywhere. Susan was welcoming, though. "Your foster mum seems nice," I said.

She shrugged. "She's well paid. It's her job." She flopped onto the bed. "I'm gonna get out of here as soon as I finish school, Becs. You wait and see, I'm gonna have it all, with bells on."

I believed her. I didn't envy her exactly, but I did admire her. She wasn't my type at all, but, somehow, against the odds, we'd managed to become friends. Suzie and Kelly weren't too pleased, but, well, I reckoned I was old enough to make my own choices. And they actually stopped saying bitchy things about Jade in front of me after a bit, when I stuck up for her.

I'd been wrong about Adam fancying Jade, though. Not long afterwards, I was on my own in the library, looking for a book for some research on the Boer War, when the door opened and he came in. He often seemed to be hovering about these days, and I'd half-hoped he liked me. Then I decided he couldn't possibly be interested, and that it was because I was hanging with Jade a lot. But now Jade wasn't here, and I saw he had a book in his hand, a Harper Lee.

He came over to the history section. "Have you read this?" he asked. I shook my head and my heart did a flip. He was only lending me a book, that was all. "It's good. Borrow it if you like," he said, and I said "Thanks", and took it. Then he cleared his throat and said "Um . . . I was wondering if you'd like to go somewhere one evening. Um . . . with me."

I couldn't believe it! I almost wanted to look over my shoulder to see if Jade or someone else had come into the library. The thought of Jade reminded me of what she'd say – play it cool. So I said, as casually as I could, considering my heart was doing the tango, "Could do. Where were you thinking?"

"There's this club I go to, there's pool and stuff, and a coffee bar, and pizza as well this Friday if you want to grab something to eat. If you like."

He looked at me with his dark-brown velvet eyes and I felt as though I was drowning and thought, oh, I like, I like, although I managed to say, again quite casual, "OK, I'll give it a go." And my heart was racing, my pulses pounding, and I was thinking, oh, Adam, Adam, you don't have to ask, I'd go to the ends of the earth with you and do whatever you want.

Five

Fainting is Not Cool

REBECCA

It seemed to take an age, like one of those slow-motion movie sequences, as Jade and I crossed the waiting room and closed the door of the consulting room behind us. It closed with a snap that held an awful hint of finality, and made me feel I wanted to tug it open again and run away.

The doctor was a woman, youngish, pretty, with dark hair pulled back in a bun, and dark-rimmed glasses. She smiled at us in a preoccupied kind of way and said, "Hello, I'm Dr Green. Take a seat, please," then swivelled her chair to consult the computer screen. I was sure she must be able to hear the hammering of my heart as Jade and I sat down side by side. Not for the first time, I wished I could be more like Jade; calm, cool and collected, and never showing a trace of nerves.

The doctor seemed to be taking ages to find the notes she wanted. At one point, she turned to us. "I'm so sorry; our computer system's been playing up all morning. I'll try not to be long." She clicked the mouse and tutted, frowning. Jade and I looked at each other and she pulled a face. I tried to smile, but it didn't quite work. Once again, I cursed my over-sensitive nerves.

I glanced around the room, breathing deeply as I'd been told it has a calming effect. It was a typical doctor's consulting room, with blinds at the window which could be pulled down for privacy, a sink, a desk, an examination couch with a pristine white cover and curtains to pull around. I looked away from that quickly. I'd disliked those couches ever since I had to be held down on one as a child, while a splinter was painfully extracted from my foot.

I was beginning to feel a little sick and light-headed. I hadn't been able to face breakfast that morning, not wanting any questions from Mum about my day. I hadn't exactly lied to her, but I'd got up at the usual time like any normal school day. I hadn't dared tell her where I was really going; Jade and I were the only two who knew. So I picked up my bag and left at the usual time, calling goodbye to Mum and my little sister Clare.

I glanced at my watch. It felt like we must have been sitting there for at least ten minutes, but I saw that barely two minutes had passed. The doctor tutted and clicked some more, muttering under her breath. My phone played its little tune and I almost jumped out of my skin. I'd forgotten to switch it off before coming in. Jade did no more than raise her eyebrows. Dr Green looked at me over her glasses. "Sorry", I muttered and switched off the phone, but not before I'd had a quick look. It was a text from Adam. "Why aren't you in school? Are you OK?"

I wished I could text him back, but I couldn't. I wished I could talk to him. I wished he was here. He always had a calming influence on me. Just thinking of him, I felt myself relax a little. Adam was so amazing: the best thing that had ever happened to me. And the most interesting person, now I'd got to know him. His mind was like quicksilver, but at the same time, he had a way of putting things into their right perspective. He was gorgeous, and fit and all I ever dreamed of in a boyfriend, and I loved him to bits. I still couldn't quite get over how I landed up with him, when he could have had his pick of any of the girls in school. I knew that a lot of them were dead envious. He said he loved me too, for my mind and my caring nature and my smile.

That almost made me smile now, but not quite, because I couldn't forget that we were in a clinic, in a consulting room with a doctor who specialised in teenage pregnancy.

Dr Green sighed. "Oh, this is hopeless! So much for modern technology." She turned round to face us, taking off her glasses and looking at us properly. "I'm so sorry about that, and the wait you've had. Fortunately I do have something down on paper as well."

She consulted the notes on her desk. Suddenly, I was not feeling well at all. My empty stomach, the tension, the waiting, had got to me. "I – I'm sorry," I said shakily. "I feel a bit faint. Could – could I have a drink of water, please?"

She got up and filled a paper cup at the sink. "You do look rather pale. Have a drink and then take some deep breaths. Don't worry too much, this is quite normal. By your notes, you've seen your GP and you are about six to seven weeks pregnant. Have you been feeling sick in the mornings?"

I took a gulp of water and almost choked on it. I took a deep breath and tried to speak, but nothing came out. Dr Green's face was in front of me, looking concerned, and behind her was Jade, saying something I couldn't hear, because there was a rushing and roaring in my head and the faces before me looked as though they were swimming under water, and then I was pitching forward into darkness.

Six

First Date

REBECCA

That first date with Adam wasn't quite what I'd expected. Not that I was very clear what I *did* expect. A club, he'd said, but I'd no idea what kind of club. I thought he'd mentioned pizza, and pool. But what to wear? Dress up, or be casual? He'd never seen me in anything but school uniform or the casual jeans and tops we wore sometimes, which were a kind of uniform in themselves. I wanted to make a good impression.

In the end, I consulted Jade. She seized on my news with enthusiasm. "Well, good on you for getting him to ask you out! How did you swing that?"

"Well, I wasn't expecting it. We were just in the library, talking about books . . ."

Jade laughed out loud and slapped me on the back. We were at her place, hanging out in her room and doing homework, in between having a bit of a gab.

One thing I'd found out about Jade, she didn't run around to everyone else repeating every bit of goss, like most people did. She worked hard and kept herself to herself most of the time. She was different to other people our age. Where most of us looked at music and celebrity blogs, or in my case read a novel, she'd study websites about people who'd made it big through their own efforts. She followed a website that advised setting five points for success. Jade's five were Vision, Excellence, Single Mindedness, Passion and Determination, and she was deadly serious about following them. We were so unalike that I often wondered how on earth we'd become friends. But we had, and I trusted her. She was the only one I'd told about Adam.

"Talking about books! Only you, Becs, only you! Wouldn't the others love it if they knew, the way they drool over him! But don't worry, I won't say a word. Where's he taking you?"

"A club, he said."

"Night club?"

"They'd never let us in at our age. Don't know really. More like a sports club, probably?"

"Well, if you want help what to wear, just ask. Or you can borrow anything of mine." If only borrowing Jade's clothes would give me her looks and style and confidence! But I knew it didn't work like that.

In the end, Jade came round that Friday, to check on me when I was getting ready for the big date. I was in a state of nerves, having tried and discarded several outfits. When she came in I was trying on a short, tight mini-dress (one that a cousin had passed on to me and that I'd never worn), with heels. I'd put my hair up and put on more make-up than I usually used. Jade took one look and tut-tutted. "No, that won't do. Talk about overkill! I don't think Adam's the kind of lad who'll go for the tarty look."

Tarty was the last way I wanted to look. I was near to tears of despair. "Well then, what?"

She took over. "For a start, go and take half that slap off your face. You don't need it, you've got nice skin. Just a discreet touch. I'll sort out an outfit."

While I was removing the make-up, Jade went through my wardrobe, such as it was. She'd brought along a couple of things of her own. In the end, she got me togged up in my own white jeans, a soft black top she'd brought with her, and some discreet silver jewellery, with flat black pumps, my hair down, and a touch of pink lip-balm and mascara.

"There! Now you look fit for anything!"

I had to admit I did look nice in the full-length mirror; slim and stylish, my best points emphasised but not over the top. And I felt comfortable, and myself. It did a lot for my confidence. "Thanks, Jade,"

I said gratefully.

"Think nothing of it. Go out and knock 'em dead. And bless you, my child."

"I could have made a right fool of myself."

"No worries. Think of me when you're out having fun and I'm working on my economics assignment!"

Adam liked the way I looked too, I could see it by the way his eyes widened when he saw me. We'd arranged to meet at the corner of my road because I was shy about him coming to my house. As I reached him he said, "You look nice."

I felt myself blush, and then felt stupid for not knowing the cool way to receive a compliment from a boy. So I just said, "Thanks. So do you." And then felt stupid again, because you don't go round complimenting boys. He did look nice though, in jeans and new trainers. I was glad my coat and scarf were new, and mentally thanked Jade again for not letting me go out looking like an overdressed idiot.

We set off into town, me still wondering where we were heading. I didn't like to ask, and he didn't say. But it felt pretty good walking along with him, and I had to keep mentally pinching myself to make sure I wasn't dreaming.

It was something of a surprise when we got to the big old church in the middle of town and turned in at the gate. "This is a church," I said, and he grinned.

"Yes, I know."

I felt a flutter of panic. "I mean, I don't go to church usually. And it isn't even Sunday."

"Don't worry," he said with a grin, "we're not going in the church." He steered me round the solid grey walls that looked as though they'd stood there for hundreds of years, and through a door at the side that opened on to a flight of stone steps leading down into the depths.

"Careful on the steps," he said. "They're a bit worn in places."

I wanted to ask where we were going, but just then Adam put out a hand to steady me, and held my hand firmly until we reached the bottom. It was a great feeling, warm and safe somehow, and I missed it when he let go. He led the way from a dimly lit flagged passageway to a kind of big cellar, all lit up, and to my surprise, full of noise and chatter. There was a pool table and another for table-tennis, both occupied, and a kind of mini-kitchen area at the far end. All the people there were our age or thereabouts, some younger, some I recognised from school, boys and girls. "Welcome to the Cellar Club," said Adam. "Let's go and grab a drink first."

There were a few curious glances as we made our way over to the coffee area, and one or two said hi. I felt my cheeks grow warm again. It would be all round school on Monday that I'd been out with Adam. Well, I didn't care. The coffee seemed to be a help-yourself affair. Adam made two mugs while I just stood there, then we carried them over to one of the little tables nearby.

"We'll have a game of pool when the table's free," he said. I thanked my stars that I had a brother who'd taught me how to play pool. Sipping the coffee, I began to feel warm and relaxed.

The cellar was huge, with what seemed to be a boiler room at the far end. Along one wall, there was timber and shelving that looked as though bookshelves were in the process of being built. Adam followed the direction of my gaze. "They're planning a kind of library there. Anyone can borrow books and return them, keep them as long as they like. That's one reason I brought you here. They've asked me to choose some books, and I don't really know what most girls like to read."

"Most of the girls I know don't read that much," I said. "Apart from magazines. But I can find out a bit more if you like. What a cool idea!"

"Yeah," he said. "We could go into Ledwall and have a look round the big bookshops one weekend, if you like, do a bit of research, see what's selling well?" Walking round bookshops in the city with Adam sounded like my idea of perfection. Jade would have a laugh if she knew we were discussing books. I couldn't help grinning at the thought.

"What's funny?" asked Adam.

"Just something Jade said."

"Oh. Jiggly Jade." I'd heard the lads calling her that, but for some reason that burst my bubble.

"That's not very nice. She's got a brain as well. She's had a rough time, but she's really nice when you get to know her."

"Yeah, sorry," said Adam, looking a bit sheepish. "If you've finished your coffee, the pool table's free?"

We were on our third game of pool when a woman came down the stone steps carrying a stack of pizza boxes. Most of the kids called out, "Hi, Mary!" and she answered them by name. They clustered around when she put the boxes down on the table. "Met the delivery boy just outside," she said. "Fetch some plates, would you, Tejani?" Then she seemed to notice me for the first time. "Oh, hello, you're new here, aren't you? Adam, aren't you going to introduce us?"

She was a lady about my mum's age, pleasant looking with dark curly hair, dressed in a casual jacket and jeans with a brightly coloured scarf draped round her neck. She took off her jacket, hung it over the back of a chair, and unwound the scarf.

Adam was looking faintly embarrassed. "Hi Mum, this is Rebecca Stanhope. She's in my year at school. Rebecca, this is my mum. She's – um – the vicar's wife."

Seven

Real Family

JADE

Having a friend was something new to me, and I hardly knew what to make of it at first. I mean, everything usually comes at a price, doesn't it? There's a hidden agenda behind everything. Susan and Paul were reasonably good foster parents, but they wouldn't do it if they weren't being paid. Likewise the social workers with their fake attitudes of care and concern. I knew very well they forgot all about me at the end of the day and went back to their nice cosy lives. Teachers the same. Doctors, nurses, all the so-called "caring professionals", were doing a job that paid well, and that was it. Families washed their hands of you if you inconvenienced them, I was living proof of that. Boys wanted you for one thing. Girls wanted nothing to do with you if you were pretty, because you were a threat. And so it went on.

I considered myself fortunate to be able to see through most people and had the brain to sort myself out and make my own life plan. Most people my age seemed to have no plan at all! And if I could make use of others along the way, all the more kudos to me.

Until I met Rebecca. Try as I might, Rebecca got to me in some subtle way I couldn't work out. Rebecca had no agenda. She was shy and nervous and sensitive, all the things I considered weaknesses. People mostly liked her, though. She had friends, and didn't seem to be a loner. She was a good student and worked hard – and I did admire that.

So, strange as it seemed, Rebecca and I had become friends. I couldn't figure out how it had happened; I didn't give her much encouragement at first. Her other friends didn't like me, I could see that. Not that I cared. But, increasingly, I found that I did care about Rebecca and her opinions, though I'd never have admitted it, and found myself looking forward to the time we spent together, and seeing her smile.

Susan invited her to tea with us and clearly approved of her, and then Rebecca's mum asked me back there. I didn't know what to expect that first time. She lived in a slightly posher part of town than us, in a nice house. She had a mum, a dad, an elder brother, an eight-year-old sister, and a dog, Raffles, a golden Labrador who greeted me with enthusiasm, waving his plumy tail. I like animals. They don't let you down like people do, and I made a fuss of him, even when he slobbered over my school bag. I could see that this went down well with the rest of the family.

Rebecca's mum is a care worker and was still in her navy uniform. "Haven't had time to change," she apologised, sliding a shepherd's pie bubbling with cheese out of the oven. "I have a late shift, so not worth it really. Please sit down and make yourself at home, Jade. Becky, could you be a love and set the table?" She brushed back the hair from her eyes and gave her elder daughter a little hug as they almost collided at the cutlery drawer. Both of them laughed.

Rebecca's dad came in from work (he worked for an estate agent), and when I was introduced, made a joke about the kitchen being steamed up with so many beautiful women, and they laughed again. I looked away when her dad gave her mum a kiss on the cheek, and teased little Clare about her topknot hairstyle. I hadn't been in a house with a real family for a long time.

Rebecca's brother, David, came in from college as we were just sitting down to the meal at the kitchen table. He wasn't a lot like Rebecca to look at; he was tall and athletic. Rebecca had told me he played rugby for the local team. His hair was fair with a bit of wave in it, his eyes blue/grey. But when he smiled I could see the likeness to his sister, the same warmth. We were introduced, and from that very first moment, David couldn't keep his eyes off me. He wasn't as obvious about it as most lads, but I was aware that he was conscious of me the whole time as we ate and chatted.

Susan and Paul didn't do a lot of banter, as the TV was mostly on in our house and the boys made a constant racket, but Rebecca's family all teased each other and laughed a lot. They seemed relaxed and comfortable with each other – even Rebecca was different than she was at school; she lost her shyness and nervousness.

And the brother . . . over apple pie and custard I toyed with the idea of getting to know him better. Not for a serious relationship, of course. That didn't fit in with my current plan. But it might be nice to have a boyfriend again, even if just for a while. It was a long time since the last one, and that had ended up messy when he started to get too possessive. I stole a glance at David, and yes, he was looking at me, and when he saw I'd noticed, he smiled that sweet smile. He had long eyelashes like Rebecca's. It might be fun, even a bit of a challenge, to get closer to him.

But then there was Rebecca. Would it spoil our friendship if I started going out with her brother? I certainly saw less of her since she'd taken up with Adam . . . Not that she was any different to me, just not around so much. But if it was me and David . . .

I jumped, suddenly aware that he was speaking to me.

"Do you play any sport, Jade?"

"Not really," I replied, and he looked a little disappointed.

"We're not all sports nuts like you," said Rebecca, and gave him a dig in the ribs.

He gave her a dig back. "Better than always having your head stuck in a book," he said, and they both smiled their heart-stopping smiles.

I thought quickly. "I quite like watching sport though," I said, and he seemed to brighten. I almost wished I hadn't said that; nothing more depressing in my opinion than standing in some muddy field watching guys chase after a ball.

I wondered if he'd say more, but he didn't. Rebecca's mum was collecting up the pudding plates and her dad was making coffee. Afterwards I helped Rebecca load the dishwasher while her mum got ready for her work shift, then the two of us went upstairs to do homework in her rather messy bedroom full of Clare's dolls and stuffed animals as well as Rebecca's stuff. David was in the hall as we passed, clipping on the dog lead to take Raffles for a walk. I allowed myself a glance over my shoulder as we headed for the stairs. He didn't look up. Still, he wouldn't forget me in a hurry. He'd be there if I wanted to take things further.

Eight

The Vicar's Son

REBECCA

I have to admit I was totally gobsmacked that day I met Adam's mum and found out she was a vicar's wife, which meant his dad had to be a vicar. I'd never met a vicar before and I didn't know anything about them. If I'd thought about it at all, I'd have imagined them to be grey-haired and very serious and studious, wearing black maybe. I couldn't imagine them to be someone with a family, someone's dad. Adam's.

Adam seemed a bit sheepish about the whole thing.

"Why didn't you tell me your dad was a vicar?" I asked after that first evening, when we were walking home together.

I suppose I was a bit embarrassed about it," he admitted. "I mean, it's not the kind of thing most people's dads do, is it?"

"Does it mean you have to go to church all the time?" I asked.

"I don't *have* to go. But I do, mostly, because Mum and Dad like me to."

I thought again what a nice person he was. Most kids our age only want to do their own thing, never mind what their family wants. "Your mum seems quite normal," I said, thinking of the person I'd just met, in her jeans and trainers, dishing out pizza and playing table tennis. He laughed.

"She is normal. We're a normal family, except we live in a vicarage. Freezing old place. It's OK though. Loads of space."

"Are there more of you?"

"Just me." He was silent for a moment, as though wondering whether to say more, then seemed to make up his mind. "Actually, that's why Mum does what she does, kind of."

I looked up at him, wondering what he meant, and he caught my eye. I didn't say anything, and after a while he went on slowly, choosing his words carefully. "Why she works with young people, I mean. There were more of us. Twins, girls, six years younger than me. They both had this thing wrong with them. A rare condition that can't be cured. Both of them died. Tilly when she was three, Anna when she was four. We still miss them . . ."

He paused, and I had the feeling that he was very near to tears. He cleared his throat. My heart went out to him, but I couldn't speak; I couldn't imagine how hard it must be to talk about something so horrendous. Suppose it had been our Clare? With a lump in my throat I reached out and took his hand, and didn't even care if it looked pushy. We just kept walking, still holding hands. There was a touch of frost now that winter was approaching, and our breaths made white clouds in the cold air. He cleared his throat again and said, "Mum had a kind of breakdown after Anna died. Wouldn't talk, wouldn't go out. It was awful." I imagined him, a nine or ten-year-old boy, having to watch his mother suffer, but still needing her himself.

I squeezed his hand. "I'm sorry."

"Yes – well – after a bit people stopped coming to see us. Even people from the church. Dad was so busy, had to keep going, everybody depended on him. Him and Mum ended up hardly talking to each other and I was really scared they were going to split up. But there was this one couple who kept coming. They never gave up. They sat with us, and talked with Mum, and cried when she cried. And prayed. They always prayed."

"And she got better?" Daft question, obviously she did.

He nodded. "Yes. It took time, but she got back to normal. She was happy again, really happy. She said that God had become more real to her than ever before, and it was going to be OK. And it was. She started doing stuff again, and Dad and her were getting along again, and then a year or so after, she said she wanted to serve God full time, so started training to work with young people. She'd been a librarian before. She worked in another youth club for a while, and now she's got her own." He stopped, looking suddenly embarrassed at revealing so much personal family stuff.

I didn't quite know what to say, so we walked in silence, but neither of us took our hands away. It felt warm and friendly, the way it had when he helped me down the steps. "Do you believe in all the God stuff yourself?" I asked after a while.

"Not sure really. I mean, I can see what a difference it made to Mum, and Dad as well, although of course I've always heard about God and the Bible. I think I do believe it when I listen to one of Dad's sermons in church. Sometimes, anyway. Or the talks Mum gives to the kids. But I can't get my head round a God who lets terrible things happen. Like my sisters dying. I don't understand how Mum and Dad can accept that. And then I think, there's no real proof anyway. I mean, was Jesus who Mum and Dad say he was, the son of God dying to save the world? Or was he just a good man from history? There've been plenty of good men, like Ghandi, and Martin Luther King, or that guy Atticus Finch."

"Atticus Finch wasn't real, that was fiction," I pointed out.

"Yes, I know, but who's to say the Bible isn't all fiction?" I had no answer to that. I couldn't believe we were having such a serious discussion on our first time out together. Jade would have laughed her socks off.

"Anyway, I think the Cellar Club is a cool place," I said, trying to lighten up a little. "Good fun as well. Your mum's idea, you said?"

"Yes, she was concerned about kids hanging round with nothing to do. Glad you liked it. I wasn't sure when I asked you."

"I did."

"Good." We seemed to have run out of things to say again, but it didn't matter, because we'd reached our gate. I could see the lighted window downstairs, which meant that my dad would still be watching telly, though my mum wouldn't be back from her late shift yet.

"Er, would you like to come in for a coffee?" I asked, and then thought how stupid it sounded, because we'd been drinking coffee all evening. My shyness seemed to have returned. I wondered if he'd try to kiss me goodnight and what it would be like. But he didn't, just gave my hand a squeeze.

"Better not, thanks. Maybe another time. I'll text you. See ya."

And he was gone, back the way he came, disappearing into the darkness. I stood for a moment, trying to get my thoughts in order before going in. Not what I'd expected from a first date. Was I disappointed? Maybe a little, because I'd half hoped he'd suggest we met over the weekend. Excited? Not exactly, although I supposed I'd wanted him to fall as madly in love with me as I was with him, and we'd seemed more like just good mates hanging out. Surprised? Yes, I was still trying to process the things he'd told me on the way home, about his family, and his mum and dad, and God and everything.

I found myself grinning suddenly. I bet he'd never talked like that to any other girl. He must think I'm special. And he'd thought I looked nice! He hadn't only asked me out just because of the books . . . I was still standing there when my mum came along the pavement, home from her evening shift. "Hello love. What are you doing standing there?"

"Just thinking."

She linked her arm in mine. "Well, come and do it inside in the warm. Where did you go this evening? Cinema? Coffee shop? I hope Adam behaved properly."

"He did, Mum," I said. "He's nice." To put it mildly, I thought, taking off my coat and unwinding my scarf in the warm hallway. He is gorgeous. He's kind, he's thoughtful, he is absolutely wonderful. And I think – I hope – he's going to be mine.

My phone buzzed. It was him, texting as he'd promised. "*I had a great time, let's do it again. Good night, sleep tight.*"

Yes, I'd had a great time too.

Nine

Model School

JADE

I pride myself on never making mistakes. Control, that's the secret. Whatever you do, make sure you're the one in control. I was pushed about when I was little; I couldn't do anything about it then. But as soon as I was able to suss out how things worked, I'd made up my mind that I would take control of my own life and make sure it stayed that way.

It was surprisingly easy, actually. I was a pretty child, even at the stage when most kids' front teeth were too big and their faces hadn't quite caught up. And I knew how to get what I wanted. I found that if I fixed the current case worker with my big brown eyes and put on a tremulous little smile, I could get them not only to listen, but to act upon whatever I put into their minds. Some of them saw through me, a lot didn't, but mostly I could work things to my best advantage.

Susan and Paul were easy to deal with. They were mostly so easy-going that I could pretty much wind them round my little finger. I'd even heard them congratulating themselves after I'd been there a couple of weeks, on how well it was all working out and what a lovely girl I was, and how they just couldn't understand why I'd been labelled as someone with problems. Well, all to the good. I wasn't going to do anything at this stage to rock the boat. I'd pretty much got over the do-everything-they-tell-you-not-to-do phase, now that I had my life plan sorted. Next year I'd start looking at uni courses, then the world was going to be falling at my feet.

However, in the meantime, this was a quiet little town with not a lot of distractions apart from studying, so, when I saw a Saturday modelling course mentioned at a college in Ledwall, our nearest big city, I looked up the online link. The course was just about to start, and ran until Christmas.

I mentioned it to Susan and showed her the website. She peered at the details. "Well, it looks all genuine and above board. Is modelling what you really want to do though? It's a lot of hard work, and you hear about some dodgy people in the business. You've got the looks, but you've got brains as well. You could do anything you chose."

"I know," I said. "It would only be a kind of sideline. I don't want to spend the rest of my life strutting up and down a catwalk. But it might be fun to do the course. It would look good on my CV and I could earn a bit of extra money modelling."

She hummed and hah-ed a bit, consulted with Jasmine, and finally said she'd come with me to the interview as she wanted to do a bit of shopping. Well, it was better than catching the bus, so we arranged it. I didn't even object when she came to the college with me and gave the woman in charge a bit of a grilling. I'd intended to lie about my age, to say I was eighteen at least, but my correct d.o.b. was noted down. I was enrolled and we had a coffee in the cafeteria. I hoped she wouldn't insist on coming with me on Saturdays, and breathed a sigh of relief when she didn't, and let me go on the bus.

The first session was reasonably interesting, mostly talks about body structure and body shapes and deportment. There were seven other girls on the course, some tall and slim, one or two were so plain and ordinary that I doubted they'd ever make it as fashion models. Or any other kind, come to that. Most of us had coffee together after that first session – I wouldn't have bothered, but I had nearly an hour to wait for my bus.

One of the girls, Jane, was real model material, so tall and skinny that her bones stuck out. Not exactly pretty, but it's amazing what make-up can do. I noticed that she didn't have milk or sugar in her coffee, and passed up the cakes and muffins the rest of us had. She was dead serious about a career in fashion modelling.

"I'm going to the top," she told us that first day. "This is just the start for me. Look out, Julia Bergshoeff and Clemence Poesy. It's going to be Janine Alexis, supermodel."

"Is that really your name?" asked one of the others.

"No, but Jane Ash doesn't have quite the same ring." She looked critically at the rest of us, stuffing our faces with chocolate chip muffins. "You girls will have to cut down on the calories", she said. "You're never gonna make it with all that flab."

None of us could be called flabby, but maybe none of us took the whole thing as seriously as Jane. She was as determined as I was to get to the top of the tree. Mind you, I'd never have done anything as stupid as starving myself in the process. That's just craziness. What's the point of getting to the top if your health is ruined and you can't enjoy it when you get there?

A couple of weeks into the course I noticed a small group of people sitting at the side of the hall at a table, with iPads to hand. "Talent scouts!" hissed Jane. "People from modelling agencies looking for promising talent. Wish I hadn't had that yoghurt for breakfast. It's gonna show." She patted her stomach area, so flat it was almost concave.

The rest of us rolled our eyes, but I watched the scouts out of the corner of my eye as we listened to our tutor and practised our walking and turning. They were watching us, and tapping away on their iPads. I gave it everything I had. This could be the beginning of something good, I thought.

There was a buzz of excitement over coffee. The talent scouts were having coffee too, at a table the other end of the hall. "That grey-haired lady is from the Martha Scott agency," said Jane, who made it her business to know all about these things. "I hope, I hope, I hope she's noticed me. It's one of the top ones."

One of the scouts was a young, good-looking man, probably in his mid to late twenties. I'd noticed him watching me, more than Jane, actually, though I didn't say so. "Who's the young guy?" I asked casually.

"I'm pretty sure he's the son of the boss of Chiltern's," said Jane. "I've seen his photo in their mag."

"Not the Chiltern's, that posh chain?"

"Yes. Didn't you know? I've been told that we're to do a charity fashion show at Christmas, and that Chilterns allow us to model the latest stuff from their store here in Ledwall. They do it every year apparently, it's in the brochure if you can be bothered to read it. It's good publicity for them. Maybe he's here looking for models for their TV ads! Now that would be a . . . eek! Don't look now, but he's coming over. My hair's OK, isn't it?"

We assured her it was perfect. The young man came over, and, yes, he was headed for our table. He had dark hair and was very tanned as though he'd had a recent sunshine holiday, and wore a pale blue cashmere sweater, casual jeans, leather loafers, a Rolex watch. He smiled and said, "Hi, ladies. Mind if I join you? My name's Henry Chiltern."

An excited but muted twitter assured him we didn't mind at all. He pulled up a chair to our table, and Jane shuffled hers up closer to Maya to make room for him. He didn't appear to notice, bringing his chair over to my side of the table and sitting down next to me.

Ten

Not According to the Plan

REBECCA

I woke in the recovery position on the floor, and groggily turned my head to see two faces looking down at me, the doctor's and Jade's, both looking concerned. The doctor was kneeling at my side.

"OK, Rebecca?" she asked. "Feeling better?"

I nodded my head and tried to sit up. What I felt was foolish with a big F. Fainting is so totally not cool. The doctor helped me up and sat me in the chair.

"Take it easy," she said. "A few deep breaths. That's it. I'm guessing you skipped breakfast, right?"

I nodded again. I hadn't even stopped for a cup of tea. I was beginning to feel better, but still a little shaky. The doctor asked about my general health, whether I was anaemic, diabetic, any other problems? I shook my head.

"Low blood sugar," said the doctor. She filled my water glass again, then opened a desk drawer and took out a paper-wrapped cereal bar. "There, eat that. And when you get out of here, go and get yourself a proper breakfast, OK?"

I said I would, and munched on the cereal bar. It did seem to settle my stomach, and my nerves, a bit. Jade handed me a tissue to wipe my sticky hands, and then sat down on the other chair, took hold of my hand and gave it a squeeze. "What are you like, Becs?"

I managed a weak smile. Some support I'd turned out to be, passing out before we'd even started. She kept hold of my hand, though, whether for my sake or her own I couldn't be sure.

The little crisis over, Dr Green became her former brisk, business-like self. "I'm so sorry for getting the two of you mixed up. Now, Jade, you're six to seven weeks pregnant, right?"

Jade nodded. "Yes."

"And your family know about it?"

"I don't have a family. Not a real family. I'm fostered."

"I see." The doctor made some notes. "And the father?"

I felt Jade's fingers stiffen against my own. "What about him?"

"Has he been told? Is he involved?"

Jade shook her head. "No, he hasn't been told. And no, he's not involved," she said and then added, very quietly, "he's married."

I thought, yes, and he's a total rat, although I didn't say anything. It had only been a couple of weeks since Jade told me everything. I could tell she was angry with herself, though she didn't want to show it. This was totally not part of her plan and it was the only time I'd ever seen her lose her cool. I couldn't believe she'd never even dropped a hint to me about it all before.

"He said he'd help me with the modelling thing," she had told me one evening when we should have been studying. "He said that with my looks and figure, and a word in his father's ear, I could become Chiltern's next Face of the Year for their advertising campaign. I told him that it wasn't the modelling I was aiming for, it was a lot higher than that, that I eventually intended to be in his father's position, or even bigger, to own my own fashion empire, at the least. He was a bit gobsmacked, but then he said he admired my ambition, he could help me with that too, that he knew all the right people and could use his influence. But for that we needed to get to know each other better . . ."

"And that meant sleeping with him?"

She'd nodded. "Yeah, I knew that was part of it. No big deal, though, I thought. If it got me on the right ladder, great."

"Oh, Jade. Didn't that feel awful?"

She'd shrugged. "Not really. We were using each other. We both understood that. And it was kind of fun." She sighed and looked down. "I even thought that maybe it might work out between us."

"I'm so sorry."

She gave this bitter little laugh. "Me too. The Chilterns have this big country house just outside Ledwall – it's the most fabulous mansion you could dream of, with gardens, a swimming pool, everything. You should have seen, it Becs! I used to go there with him after the modelling course. The rest of the family were in their holiday place in Florida. I never told a soul, couldn't risk it getting back to Susan and Jasmine. I kind of wanted to tell you, but I hardly knew you when I first started going, and I was so excited I didn't dare take any chances. I was going to have a place like that myself one day. Only better. And then I saw this, and I finished with him."

She'd pushed a crumpled local paper at me, with a picture of a smiling couple, a good-looking dark-haired young man and a pretty blonde girl. The caption read *"Chiltern's heir to wed Lady Cecilia Campbell, daughter of the Earl and Countess of Lathmore, at a lavish ceremony at Lathmore Castle on New Year's Eve."*

I said, "Oh, Jade. So he's married now?"

Another laugh. "Yes. What a total, stupid idiot I was. He'd been just passing the time with me while his fiancée and her family were preparing for the wedding. I never suspected anything." Suddenly her face had crumpled and she'd said, in a shaky little voice, "Rebecca, I think I'm pregnant."

All this seemed to flash through my mind in a second or two, while the doctor was silent for a moment. Then she said, "And what are your thoughts about the pregnancy, Jade? What do you want to do?"

"A termination. As soon as possible." I felt Jade's hand tremble. She had cried a little, telling me what happened, but by next day was back to her normal self, cool, calm and focused. It was a blip, and it made her feel like a fool, but it was just temporary. It could be fixed. She'd learn from her mistakes and go on with her life plan. No probs. And what was I looking so upset about? *You need to toughen up, Becs, big time, or you'll get walked all over.*

Dr Green swivelled to look into her face. "I'm afraid it's not quite that simple, Jade."

"Why not? That's what I've come here for. That's what this clinic is for."

"A lot of things have to be considered. We need to talk over all the options. You'll need some counselling sessions . . ."

I felt Jade's hand tighten and then she dropped mine and clenched both her fists. She was looking angry. "I don't need counselling! I know what I want!"

"Yes, but you also need a little time to think things through, talk it over with your foster parents maybe, and see what you're really feeling deep down."

Jade stood up and pushed back her chair so suddenly that it almost fell over. "I know what I feel. I know what I want. And if you won't do it, then I'll go somewhere else."

The doctor stood up too and put out her hand. "Jade, listen . . ."

But Jade wasn't listening to anything. She said, "Come on, Becs," picked up her bag and stormed out.

Eleven

Bad Choices

JADE

I was so mad with the doctor at the clinic, I almost knocked over a nurse in the hallway, and didn't even stop to apologise. The doctor and Rebecca were both scurrying along behind me. The doctor was saying, "Jade, wait, let's sit down and talk this through," but I took no notice, wrenching open the door and storming out.

The doctor fell back once I was out of the building. She couldn't very well grab hold of me and force me back inside. But Rebecca was there at my shoulder, almost running to keep up with me. "Jade, wait! Come back inside."

I didn't slow my pace. "No way! Call that a clinic? They're supposed to help people, not try to talk them out of things."

"She was trying to help. You didn't give her a chance.

You could at least have listened to what she was going to say."

I didn't reply for a moment. For one thing, I'd rushed so fast I'd got a stitch in my side and I was out of breath. We were half-way down the street, well away from that so-called clinic and that patronising woman. She was just like all the other patronising women I'd met in my life, the medical people, the social workers, the teachers. I stopped and flopped down on a bench, catching my breath. "I thought they'd sort it for me. That's what they're there for. I thought they might even do it right away, today. You hear of girls going in to get it done in their dinner break."

"I wouldn't have thought they'd do that. What will you do now?"

"Find somewhere else," I said. The stitch had eased and I'd got my breath back but for once I wasn't feeling all that confident. The anger had drained away and left me feeling kind of flat and a bit sick. Was it too soon for morning sickness? I knew very little about pregnancy and I didn't want to. This was definitely something I hadn't planned for. I was the one in control of my life, except suddenly I wasn't. To my horror, I felt a huge sob rise in my throat and I couldn't choke it down. I leaned forward with my head in my hands and felt the tears trickle through my fingers.

Rebecca put her arm round me and made comforting noises. A woman passing by stopped and asked, "Are you all right, dear?" and I heard Rebecca say, "Yes, yes, she's OK, thanks," and I was grateful. The last thing I wanted was nosey busybodies poking themselves into my business.

At that point, if I was Rebecca I think I'd have headed for the hills, a.s.a.p, but she was going nowhere. I raised my head and looked at her. Her face was screwed up anxiously and she was very pale. I remembered she'd only just recovered from fainting in the doctor's consulting room. She was perhaps the only real friend I had in the world. I pulled myself together.

"Becs, we'd better go and get something to eat before you pass out again. There's a sandwich bar just round the corner."

She seemed relieved that I was looking more normal, and nodded. In the sandwich bar we sat in the most private corner and warmed our hands round mugs of tea. I made Rebecca order a bacon buttie, but I couldn't face anything myself. I saw the colour come back into her face as she ate.

"What will you do now?" she asked again, when her plate was empty.

I shrugged. "Look online for another clinic, I suppose."

"Hadn't you . . . wouldn't it be better if you told Susan and Paul or your social worker? I mean, it's not like having a tooth out, is it?"

"No way. I don't want lectures, or advice. Just to get it over with."

She was looking thoughtful, drinking her second mug of tea. "Have you thought about, er – keeping it?"

"Are you crazy? Me with a baby? Totally not going to happen. And don't say a word to anyone."

"I won't," she said, and I knew she would keep her word. I could imagine what would happen if it got round school, lectures from teachers, and the kids would have a field day, calling me slut and slag and gloating over it all, saying it served me right. Which it did, in a way, I supposed, when I really thought about it.

Rebecca seemed to echo my thoughts. "What on earth were you thinking of to let it happen?"

I shrugged again. "Careless. Another bad choice. I went on the pill when I realised what that scumbag had in mind, but it takes time to work. Must have been too soon. Should have used something else but I suppose I thought I could risk it . . ."

"And you don't have any – feelings for him?"

I shook my head. "Not any more. He promised he'd help with my career and I believed him. I even thought, well, I could do worse than marry him, or at least keep a relationship going for a while. And all the time he was lying, lying to me, cheating on his fiancée. I've got a good mind to let Lady Cecilia What's-Her-Name know what a total lowlife she's marrying."

I lingered on that thought for a moment as the two of us sat there. He had an awful lot to lose, and I could really make him suffer. I could even threaten to go to the newspapers with the story unless he paid me to keep quiet. But blackmail isn't really my style, and I just wanted to forget the whole thing and move on. He'd probably deny it anyway. DNA testing could prove he was the father, but that would mean I'd have to have the baby . . . My thoughts were going in circles. Rebecca was looking at me, anxious again.

"Please don't do anything silly, will you?"

"I won't," I said. Now that the anger had drained away I felt silly anyway. Rebecca was right. I should at least have listened to what the doctor was saying. I didn't want to have to start all over again at another place. I'd have to go back and apologise. I looked at Rebecca across the table and thought; I don't know why she bothers with me really. She has everything – a real family, a nice home, a proper boyfriend. She's got brains and she's even really pretty when she makes the effort.

I looked at my watch. "If you get a move on, Becs, you can get back to school for the next lesson."

"What are you going to do?"

"Going back to the clinic."

She didn't even hesitate. "Well then, I'll come with you."

Twelve

The Film

REBECCA

It's strange how things work out. Sometimes coincidences really make you think.

After that disastrous, embarrassing morning at the clinic, I never wanted to show my face in there again. Ever. But we did go back. Jade apologised for rushing out. The doctor was kind and understanding and said she was glad we'd gone back. She was fully booked for the afternoon, but the receptionist made Jade a priority appointment for the following week. I was dying with embarrassment over fainting and Jade making a scene, but the doctor never turned a hair. She seemed so pleased we'd gone back and gave Jade some leaflets that she said might answer some of her questions.

And then, the very next evening, Mary came up to me at the Cellar Club. She'd asked me to call her

Mary; all the kids did. It seemed odd to call her that, with her being the vicar's wife and Adam's mum and everything, but after a few days it just seemed friendly and natural. She told me they were having a special evening, girls only, that Thursday, with a film and a discussion on life before birth, and would I like to go?

I felt my cheeks growing pink, and wondered if she thought Adam and I had been having sex or something, and then wanted to kick myself because it looked as though I was feeling guilty, and I wasn't. We hadn't. We talked about it, and I really did fancy him like crazy, and he felt the same about me, but we agreed we wouldn't right now, with lots of studying for exams going on. I'd seen girls get into a relationship and get so wrapped up in it that everything else went by the board. Maybe in the summer . . .

But Mary wasn't getting at us at all. When I looked at the Cellar programme, I saw that this has been scheduled for a long time, so I said I'd go. I wondered, fleetingly, whether Jade would be interested in coming with me, but I hardly dared ask her. She was back at school, acting as though everything was normal. How she managed it, I don't know, with everything that was hanging over her. So I didn't say a word.

There was a notice up in school though; Mary must have asked permission for it to be there. Anyway, there was quite a little buzz of interest around the poster, and when the evening came, I saw several girls from school there, including Suzie and Kelly, although I didn't hang around with them nearly as much as before – I didn't even know they were planning on going. They didn't like Jade, and made no secret of it.

"Where's your best friend then, Becs?" Kelly asked as we found seats, with a bit of an edge to her voice.

"Wasn't interested," I said. I didn't have long to think how mean some people can be, before the film started. I settled into the seat and prepared to watch another version of the stuff we'd gone over with Miss Brent in our Personal Development class. Pregnancy and childbirth; we'd done it all before.

But this was different. We went straight into the film, with predictable opening of a kind of huge explosion on the screen, followed by dozens of little squiggling tadpoles frantically making their way towards a huge round ball. That always caused some giggling from the girls and I could imagine the rude comments there'd have been from the boys. I was glad it was girls only. If Adam was here too I'd have got some ribbing from Suzie and Kelly.

From the very start, I was transfixed. Maybe it was seeing it all on a bigger screen, maybe it was the stirring music soundtrack that accompanied this film. I had a feeling, though, that it was the knowledge that all this was actually happening to my friend.

Almost holding my breath, I saw the drama of that fertilized egg dividing within twenty-four hours, then dividing again and again and again. I saw the beginnings of a spinal cord, a heart that pulsed with life, a formless blob taking shape as a curved body and a large drooping head.

I saw tiny outcrops that would be arms and legs, big bulging eyes that looked as though they belonged to some alien creature, little indentations that would be ears, a nose, a mouth. As the film played on, eyelids formed and covered the bulging eyes, the limbs developed and tiny protrusions of fingers and toes emerged.

I had never really taken in the extraordinary events that happen before the birth of a child – any child. By twenty-two days the heart is beating. All the internal organs are in place by week three. By week six, there are fingernails, a mouth, lips, another week and the baby is kicking and swimming about. I calculated rapidly; by Jade's appointment in a few days she'd be eight weeks. I was holding my breath when I heard that by now, the baby would have its own unique fingerprints and would be able to hear.

I felt as though I'd been kicked in the stomach. Jade's little unborn baby was already a person, with its own fingerprints. It was swimming about in there and it could hear! I wondered what sounds seemed like to it; were they muffled or far away, could it hear human voices? Had it heard us discussing its fate?

I felt sick and closed my eyes. The voice-over was describing weeks nine and ten, teeth forming, hiccups, frowning, week twelve, all parts that can experience pain complete, nerves, spinal cord, vocal cords. It can suck its thumb. There was something so beautiful about this beginning to life . . .

I couldn't cope with any more. I felt something like a sob rising in my throat. I must have made a sound, because Kelly was looking at me curiously and Suzie on her other side was peering round to look at me, too.

"Are you OK, Becs?" asked Suzie.

"It's all a bit icky, isn't it? Too much information, if you ask me," added Kelly.

"I just have a bit of a headache," I lied. "It's stuffy in here. I think I'll get some air."

"Shall I come with you?" Kelly offered, but I shook my head.

Outside the Cellar, I leaned against the wall in the dim passageway, breathing the cold air that came down the steps, and fighting the emotions that threatened to engulf me. I'd never realised how complex a human being is, how amazing and breathtaking and wonderfully a baby is put together. I'd known the basics, of course. But not what goes on in there. To me, an unborn baby was a bump, getting bigger and finally emerging as a small, pink, and often screaming baby. And Jade had one growing inside her, developing by the day. And she was planning to destroy it, a tiny little person who sucked its thumb and could hear her voice. She couldn't. I wouldn't let her.

I almost jumped out of my skin when I felt a hand on my arm. It was Mary. "Sorry," she said, "but I saw you come out and I saw you were upset. Do you want to talk about it?"

I gulped. "Yes. No. I don't know." I desperately wanted to talk to someone, but I'd promised Jade. But I had to say something, do something. And then a huge sob rose in my throat and I burst into tears.

Thirteen

The Prayer

REBECCA

I felt Mary's hand tremble, just a little, and I thought, oh no, I bet she's thinking this is all about me, that I'm pregnant, and that Adam's life will be ruined, and it's all my fault, and she's going to hate me . . .

My imagination was running away with me, big time. I took a grip on myself as Mary said, "Look, why don't you pop round to the vicarage. Adam's watching the match at his mate's, as you know, but his dad will let you in. I'll text and tell him to expect you. I'll finish up here and come as soon as I can."

I couldn't think straight, so I just said OK. I wiped my eyes, pulled myself together and went up the steps.

I'd been to the vicarage next door to the church once or twice before, with Adam, and met his dad, the vicar, a kind, quiet man with thick glasses. He seemed surprised to see me; he probably hadn't read Mary's text. "Oh, Rebecca! Adam's not here, I'm afraid, and Mary's round at the Cellar."

I explained as best I could that Mary was coming to talk to me after the film finished. He seemed faintly mystified, but asked me in and made me a coffee. Their living-room is big, and comfortable, with large squashy sofas, comfy cushions and throws, an open fire and piles of books and magazines on the coffee table. We sat and watched a documentary about Greece on TV and drank coffee for a while, not saying much. Adam's dad is not a really chatty person, and I was glad of it. He must have noticed I was upset, but he didn't ask any questions and I was grateful. To be honest I was having a hard enough time trying to hold myself together. My mind was whirling with the images I'd been watching, and the realisation of what they meant.

Mary came in after a while, bustling and breathless. "Sorry to keep you waiting. The girls had a lot of questions. Good, you've had coffee. Thanks, love," she said, to her husband. "Is it OK if Rebecca and I go through to the study?"

The vicar said it was fine. The study was quiet but a bit chilly. Mary checked the old-fashioned chunky radiator, pulled a face and picked up a red cardigan and put it on over her top. "The heating in this place is very temperamental. Must have been installed a hundred years ago. I'd keep my jacket on if I were you."

I'd had time to think while I'd been waiting. I desperately wanted to talk about Jade and the baby. Surely it wouldn't be breaking a promise if I didn't mention names? We settled into two chairs facing each other, and Mary said, "Well now, do you want to tell me why you were so upset?"

I nodded. Mary has such a nice face, a bit like Adam's; she has his eyes and his tumbling curly hair, although hers has a bit of grey in it. She waited expectantly.

"It was the film," I said slowly. "Seeing – all that. There's this person I know – a friend – not one of those there tonight though – and – she's pregnant." I paused. Mary nodded slowly. I think she'd guessed, and I was just hoping she didn't think it was me. I was blushing again, I could feel it. I floundered on. "She – she's decided to get rid of it. She has an appointment next week. But – but – now I don't think she ought to. It's – it's – like murder, almost, isn't it?"

There was a sudden loud clanking from the radiator, and I jumped. "Don't worry," said Mary, "it's just coming to life. It'll warm up now."

Mary didn't speak again for a moment, but sat looking thoughtful and serious.

"How far along is your friend?"

"About seven to eight weeks, I think."

"How has her family taken it?"

"She doesn't have a family, not really. She's fostered."

"I see. Has she told her social worker?"

"No. She won't tell anyone."

"And is she in a relationship?"

"No. Not any more."

"Does the boy know about it?"

I shook my head, thinking about Henry Chiltern. "No. It's – complicated."

"He ought to be told."

"She doesn't want to tell him. She just wants it to be – all over with, and to get back to normal."

She was silent for a moment. "And what do you think?"

The radiator had certainly come to life, I was feeling too warm now. "Well, I don't know. I suppose I thought it would be better to just – you know, get rid of it. But now . . . I don't know. I thought it would just be a mass of cells . . ."

Mary shook her head. "A lot of people think that. That's why I wanted to show the film, so that girls know just what happens when someone gets pregnant. It's quite amazing, isn't it, to realise just how human an unborn child is, right from the start?"

"A heartbeat at twenty-two days," I said, marvelling at the thought. Then I felt my eyes fill with tears again. "I can't let Jade do it, I can't." And then I realised what

82

I'd done, I'd mentioned Jade's name. Mary didn't turn a hair though. I guess vicars and their wives hear all kinds of things they have to keep to themselves. She leaned forward and patted my knee reassuringly. "Nothing we say will go any further than this room, so don't worry."

"But what can I do? She's made up her mind." I imagined Jade laughing her head off if I suggest she keep the baby. *In your dreams, Becs! Not part of my plan.*

Mary was thoughtful again. "In the long run, I'm not sure at the moment, Rebecca. You sound as though you're a good friend and one who sticks by a mate. But there is one thing we can do, right here and now. We can pray."

I remembered Adam saying that his mother had found God after losing her two little girls. She'd certainly been through some pain herself. But I was doubtful. She'd said *we* can pray, not just her. "I, I don't really know how to pray."

"It's just like talking to God. It *is* talking to God. Don't worry, I'll do the talking. But before we do, I'd like to show you something."

She got up and picked up a book that had been lying on the desk. I saw that it said *Youth Bible* on the cover. She leafed through the pages. "Ah, here we are. Psalm 139. *'You made my whole being; you formed me in my mother's body. I praise you because you made me in an amazing and wonderful way. What you have done is wonderful. I know this very well. When I was put together there, you saw my body as it was formed. All the days planned for me were written in your book before I was one day old.'"* She closed the Bible, put it down and took off her glasses. "How about that, then? Isn't that just something? Our lives all planned out by God, even before we were born."

"Wow." I didn't know what else to say. I didn't know there were things like that in the Bible. Things that mattered now.

"So you see, every life is precious, and planned, and hasn't just happened by chance. Even when it all seems a big mistake. God can turn everything around and make even bad things come out good."

This was all a bit much to take in. I needed time to think, but I think I nodded.

"So," said Mary. "Let's ask God what's best for your friend and her baby, and ask him to guide us."

I wondered if we'd have to kneel down and put our hands together before we prayed, but Mary just leaned forward and took my hand and spoke in the same voice she'd been talking to me in, not like a vicar's wife's voice at all. I can't remember the exact words, but it was something like, "Dear God, thank you for Rebecca and the way she cares about her friend. Please help her friend to make the right decisions about her baby. Guide us in what we say or do. And thank you that you love us all so much. Amen."

That's all. No big drama or pleading or ranting, more like asking someone for help, and trusting they would know what to do.

She gave my hand a squeeze and smiled at me, and suddenly I felt this lightness, as though somebody had taken a load from my shoulders, and I didn't want to cry any more. Even my nerves had settled a bit, and I wanted to give Adam's mum a big hug. But I was still a bit too shy to do that, so I just said "Thank you!"

Fourteen

A Difference of Opinion

JADE

It seemed endless, waiting for the next week to come, and my appointment. I was back at school and things were going on much as usual. Except they weren't. For the last few days, I'd noticed I was having to go to the toilet a lot more than usual, it seemed like almost every hour. I wondered if I had an infection, and if I ought to see the doctor and get antibiotics or something. I was even having to excuse myself in the middle of lessons sometimes. I didn't normally do embarrassment, not like poor Rebecca, but it was beginning to make me feel uncomfortable, walking in and out of class. And then I read on some pregnancy website that the enlarging uterus presses on the bladder and makes it more sensitive. I could do without that.

I wished I hadn't stormed out of that clinic and made the whole process stretch out another week. It might already have been all over. And I wished I'd never set eyes on Henry Chiltern. Still, although things weren't going my way just now, in a week or so I'd get my life back on track, so I thought.

Then Susan pounced on me one morning. I think it was the Friday. "Are you OK, Jade? I heard you getting up in the night. And I must say you're looking a bit peaky this morning. You're not eating much breakfast. Have you picked up a tummy bug or something?"

I pushed away my half-eaten slice of toast and nodded. Truth to tell, I was feeling queasy in the mornings these days.

"I think the lasagne at school was a bit dodgy. Might be a bit of food poisoning."

"Oh dear! I'd better ring the school and inform them. I wonder if anyone else has been taken ill?"

Aagh, I should have known she'd react like that. The boys were flicking crumbs at each other but she was ignoring them, fishing out her phone already, searching through it for the school number.

"Don't ring them," I said quickly. "I've just remembered I got a pie on the way home from Rebecca's. It did taste a bit off. But I'm fine to go to school."

"Better to avoid those pies, you never know what goes into them," said Susan. But she put the phone away and started to sort out the boys and I got out of the house with a sigh of relief.

Rebecca was behaving a bit oddly that morning. She seemed kind of preoccupied, and was biting her nails again, I noticed. Since I gave her a manicure and painted them for her, she seemed to have dropped that habit. But there she was, nibbling away again.

"Have you and Adam fallen out or something?" I asked as we headed out of class to our first lessons. She looked blankly at me. "No, why?"

"You just seem worried." She was quiet for a moment, then opened her mouth to say something, but at that moment, Kelly called across to her, with a sly little grin. "OK now, Becs?"

She jumped. "Yes, I'm fine."

"Only I wondered, after you left the film last night." She exchanged a grin with Suzie, then went on, "It's OK, we won't spread it around. And we're here for you if you want to talk."

She sounded so false and smarmy that I wanted to punch her. What on earth was she talking about? I raised my eyebrows and looked at Rebecca, but she was carefully tying her laces and didn't look up. Her hair was falling forward and mostly hiding her face, but what I could see of it had gone a bit pink. What was going on?

Rebecca wasn't telling me anything, but I kept my eyes and ears open, and later in the afternoon overheard a whispered conversation in a group of some of the other girls. They shut up when they saw me, but I'd heard enough for light to dawn. For some unknown reason, they thought that Rebecca was pregnant.

I tackled her about it when we were alone, walking home from school. She went red and then white, but she didn't seem surprised. She said, "I guessed that's what they were getting at. It's because I got upset at a film we saw at the Cellar Club, about – about life before birth. I've got a steady boyfriend, they've put two and two together and made five."

I stopped in my tracks. "They think you're pregnant?" Oh my goodness, that was going to be all round school! Poor Becs.

She looked at me. "Thing is, somebody from school saw us going into that clinic as well. That's proof in their eyes."

"Why didn't you say something?"

"How can I, without everything coming out? About you, I mean."

Unexpectedly, my eyes filled with tears. She'd let herself be put in the firing line to shield me. I didn't know what to say, so I said the first thing that came into my head. "What does Adam say? Will he think it's true – about you?"

"No, of course not. We haven't – you know . . . and I haven't told him about you."

I started walking again. This kind of rumour takes off like wildfire and won't die down until something else comes along. If only . . .

Rebecca gave a kind of gulp, and said, "There's something else. That film – it showed you all the different stages. Jade, your baby's got a heartbeat, it's got all its fingers and toes, it's moving around, it can feel pain."

I stared at her. I wasn't sure I believed what she was saying, and I didn't want to hear it anyway. "No, I'm not eight weeks yet. It's just a mass of cells; it's not even really human yet."

"It is! It really is! It's a person, and it's growing every day, and it can hear and everything. You – you – can't do it! You can't kill it . . ." We'd stopped again, standing on the pavement and hissing at each other in stage whispers, although there was no one else around.

My heart was beginning to pound uncomfortably and I was feeling sick again. "Shut up, Becs. I don't believe all that stuff, and anyway, it's my decision, my body and my life and I can do what I like with it."

Rebecca was almost in tears. I'd never seen her this upset over anything. I hadn't expected all this. And she wasn't ready to give up. "Yes, but there's someone else involved as well – the baby."

"Don't call it that! It's just a foetus. Anyway, I don't care what you say. I'm going back to the clinic next week and arranging everything. You needn't come. You needn't have anything to do with it. In fact, I'd rather you didn't."

I heard her sob as I turned and ran off, leaving her standing there, properly in tears now. She'd been a good friend, maybe the only real one I'd ever had, but I could do without her, especially if she was turning all goody-goody and preachy on me. She didn't need me, she had Adam and a nice family and a lovely life. And I didn't need her.

She didn't come after me, and I didn't look back. It was beginning to drizzle, and I could easily convince myself that the dampness on my own cheeks was just raindrops.

Fifteen

A Close Thing

REBECCA

I was still upset when I met Adam later in the evening. I was worried, too. I wondered if he'd heard that stupid rumour that was going round. But he seemed the same as usual. He noticed that I was a bit off though.

"Are you OK, Becs? You're a bit quiet."

It was a lovely fresh evening after the rainy spell and we'd decided to go for a walk down by the river while it was still daylight. We'd got chips and eaten them on the bench by the water. There were puddles along the river path, and at one of them a mother duck was introducing her babies to the joys of water. They were still all yellow and downy and cute, but they were fast learners and just loved the water, dabbling their beaks into it and then standing up and comically flapping their tiny little wings. The mother seemed to be pleased they were enjoying themselves, quacking encouragingly.

"I'm OK," I said. "Had a bit of a fall-out with Jade, that's all. We disagreed about something."

He didn't ask what, but gave my hand a comforting squeeze. "It'll all come right." We left the ducks to their puddle and walked on, holding hands. Adam was so comfortable to be with. I was so lucky to have him as a boyfriend. My heart seemed to lift and give a little skip of joy. It was almost spring, we were in love, and life was wonderful. Then I remembered Jade, and that it wasn't so wonderful for her, and that we didn't seem to be friends any more. The short-lived burst of joy dissolved into sadness. Adam squeezed my hand again. "Do you want to go to the Cellar for a coffee?"

I shook my head. "I'd rather not be around other people at the moment. Can we go round to yours for a bit?"

"If you like."

Dusk was falling now and there were no lights on at the vicarage. Adam let us in with his key. "Almost forgot. Dad's away at a conference and Mum's doing the pizza thing at the Cellar. We've got the place to ourselves."

He went to switch on the living-room light. Evenings were still chilly, but the fire was lit, glowing warmly behind the spark guard, and the room looked cosy and inviting. I said quickly, "Don't put the light on. It's nice like this."

He removed the guard and put another log on the fire, which crackled and blazed up, sending flickering shadows over the hearthrug and squashy sofas. I sank into the one facing the fire with a sigh.

"Coffee?" asked Adam. I didn't really want coffee, just to sit here with Adam and forget my troubles for a while. We cuddled up together, I closed my eyes and for the first time today I felt relaxed. When Adam pulled me close and started to kiss me, it felt so right, so comforting . . .

"Becs," he said, and his voice sounded kind of husky. He was breathing fast, and his hand was stroking my neck and then moving downward to undo the next buttons of my shirt. He kissed my throat, and my hands were burying themselves in his lovely springy, curly hair and holding him close. He pulled away for a moment, breathing hard. "Becs, you know we said we wouldn't . . ."

I felt myself being carried along on a wave of love and longing and excitement, and I heard myself murmuring, "But we can change our minds, can't we?" and he was saying "Becs, I love you so much . . ."

And then a headlight beamed through the window and came slicing across the far wall until it came to rest. Adam groaned. "My dad! I thought he wasn't home until tomorrow."

We just had time to pull ourselves together and

smooth our ruffled hair. By the time Adam's dad came in, wearing his dog collar and blinking a little in the light of the table lamp we'd quickly switched on, we were sitting decorously on the sofa, not too close, apparently studying the TV guide and trying to decide whether to watch a comedy or go to the movie channel. I felt so guilty I'm sure it must show. I'd been leading Adam on, we could easily have gone too far and the rumour going round school might have come true. I hadn't fully realised how easy it would be to let that happen.

"Hello, you two," said Adam's dad cheerily, dumping down his briefcase and coming to warm his hands at the fire. "Brr – touch of frost tonight I think. Everything OK?"

Of course we said everything was fine. Adam's dad said he was going to take a quick shower and change, and departed upstairs. I stood up, too.

"I think I'll go home and get an early night."

Adam looked puzzled. "Are you OK? It's really early yet. And I'm sorry about – before."

"It's OK. I have a bit of a headache."

"I'll come with you."

But I wanted to be alone, to think. "Don't worry. There's street lights all the way. I want to be on my own for a bit. I'll text when I get there."

And I grabbed my coat and left. I did need time to

think, to be alone, to try and process the events of the day. To come to terms with losing Jade as a friend, and to realise just how easy it would be to let my feelings for Adam carry me – or both of us – beyond the barriers of reason and conscience. I could easily be that girl they thought I was at school. And part of me was still wishing that Adam's dad hadn't come home just then. I remembered Adam's gentle kiss on my neck and the warmth of his hands . . . surely it couldn't be wrong to make love when you really and truly cared for each other as Adam and I did? We hadn't given a thought to what the consequences might be though. Not a single thought. It was all too much. For the second time today, I was going home with tears pouring down my face.

There was another shock in store on Monday morning. I turned up with some trepidation, and a cold lump of sadness somewhere deep inside. I'd texted Jade over the weekend, but she hadn't replied, so it looked like our friendship was well and truly over. Plus I was worried about the gossip that was going round, and how I'd cope.

Jade didn't even glance at me when she came into the classroom, or not that I noticed. She looked as cool and elegant as ever, never a hair out of place. She went over and had a word with Mr Phelps. He looked rather startled, but nodded his head. Jade sat near the front, where she'd sat on that first day, not next to me, and again I felt a cold clutch of emptiness and loss.

After registration, Mr Phelps stood up and said, "Could you just wait a moment before going to your classes, please? Jade has something she wishes to tell you all."

I felt my heart begin to race. What was this?

Jade stood facing us, not looking at me or anyone else, but gazing steadily in front of her. I saw that there were faint dark shadows under her eyes. "There's something I want you all to know. This rumour has been going round for a few days, that Rebecca is pregnant. It's not true. One of you may have seen us coming out of the clinic in Ledwall, but it wasn't for her. It was me. I'm pregnant, but it will all be sorted out this week. Just so you know."

Her voice ended in a slight quiver. There was a stunned silence across the room, followed by a few smothered giggles, and a bit of shuffling and smirking among the lads. I didn't know what Adam must be thinking or making of it all, and I didn't dare look at him. I did look at Jade though, and as she turned to pick up her bag she met my eyes, and I knew that this had been unbearably hard for her, and that she had done this brave and extraordinary thing for my sake, and mine alone.

Sixteen

For Rebecca

JADE

I knew that my announcement would cause a stir, but I wasn't prepared for the massive can of worms that I had opened. I was slightly amazed at what I'd done; I certainly hadn't planned on spilling my guts to the whole school, but one look at Rebecca's pale, sad little face that Monday morning and I knew I had to do it. She would so hate it, everyone whispering about her in corners, calling her names, maybe bullying her. She's so super-sensitive and nervous that I was afraid she just wouldn't be able to take it. So I had to set the record straight. After all, that's what friendship is for, right?

We weren't even half way through first period when I was called to the Head's office. Phelps must have informed him straight away. I prepared myself for a grilling. I wasn't expecting to see Susan and Paul there too, but there they both were, looking well peeved, sitting waiting for me with Mr Miller, the Head. Mr Miller waved me to another chair. "Sit down, Jade." He cleared his throat. I wondered if he had a standard little lecture for girls in my situation. But before he could say much of anything, Susan burst into tears.

"This is such a shock. We've got on so well with Jade, really we have, Mr Miller, and we've had no trouble with her . . ."

Mr Miller pushed a box of tissues across the desk towards her. I could see that he was majorly disgruntled. "Jade, Mr Phelps has told me that you made an announcement to the class this morning, is it all true?" As if he thought I might be doing a drama queen thing and trying to draw attention to myself! I nodded. Susan sobbed afresh. She must have rushed straight here, she was still in her jogging bottoms and slippers, no less, and no make-up on at all. Paul looked like thunder and glared across at me, he seemed mega annoyed, probably at being pulled out of work, and that Susan was upset. I wondered if this meant I'd have to move again.

Mr Miller picked up a pencil and twiddled it. "I don't want to know all the details, Jade. Miss Fisher is our head of pastoral care; she's unfortunately not here today but will see you on her return tomorrow and go into everything with you." He paused. "And – er – when is the baby due?"

"September."

He tapped the pencil on the desk, calculating. "Our policy here is that pregnant students attend as usual, providing there are no health problems. If exams coincide with – um – delivery dates, they can be re-scheduled. But in your case, you should be able to take them as usual."

Susan was still sniffling, but she suddenly burst out with, "I'm not sure I can cope with a newborn baby as well as the twins . . ."

I was beginning to feel annoyed. They were all assuming I was going to have the baby. Nobody had asked a thing about what I wanted; what I planned to do! So I told them. "You won't have to. It's all arranged. I'm having a termination, hopefully this week."

That made them all sit up and look at me. Hadn't anyone thought of the obvious solution? They'd be contacting social services next.

"Of course, social services will have to be involved," said Mr Miller, right on cue, and Paul chipped in, "We'll ring Jasmine today."

I groaned inwardly. More interference. Why hadn't I kept my mouth shut this morning? I could have waited another week and it would all be over. But that wouldn't have helped Rebecca. I was beginning to feel sick again and I had a headache. I wanted to get out of there. "I don't feel very well," I said. "I feel a bit sick."

Mr Miller looked alarmed. Obviously he didn't want

pregnant schoolgirls throwing up over his neat and tidy study. He got to his feet. "I suggest you take the rest of the day off, Jade, and that we all take time to consider the way forward. Then we can speak again in the near future."

I got up and left, Susan following me. Paul stopped to exchange a few words with Mr Miller. Susan had stopped sniffing and put her arm round me. It was strangely comforting. They shepherded me out of school and into the car, not saying much, thankfully. I wondered again if we would soon all be parting company.

Back home, Paul, still tight-lipped, returned to work and Susan suggested I go back to bed. I was quite glad to get to my room and lie down. I really was feeling tired and ill. Truth to tell, this hadn't been the best morning. I could feel things slipping out of my control, but deep down, I wasn't sorry I did what I did. It must have been a relief for Rebecca.

It was quite comforting to get into my pyjamas and crawl back under the duvet. It must have been Susan's cleaning day, there was a hoover parked in the middle of the floor. After a bit, she appeared in the doorway. "Can I bring you something to eat? Cup of tea or some soup or something?"

I didn't fancy anything. What I wanted to do was sleep. I yawned. "Not really, thanks. Maybe later."

She went, taking the hoover with her. I thought

about Susan; she was sometimes irritating, and tended to get stressed out with the two boys as well as me to cook and clean for, but she had a kind side to her as well. I had my own room here, with a lock on it to keep the boys out, and I'd been a fool to mess up on this placement. The sick feeling was subsiding, although I felt a bit achey. It started to rain, a cold sleety rain that made scratching sounds against the window. I was warm, the bed was comfortable, the house was quiet, and I slept.

My dreams were muddled though. Rebecca was in them, and she was crying. Then Jane from modelling class was there and she was crying, too. Susan was crying, and Henry Chiltern was coming in and looking at his watch and saying time was running out, because he was getting married.

Somewhere in the distance there was a baby crying, and that became a nightmare. I had to stop it crying like that, but I couldn't. I was searching and searching but couldn't find it.

I woke with a start; the boys were home from school and I heard their voices downstairs and a door slamming. Susan must have shushed them because things went quiet and I drifted back into sleep. But not for long. There was this nagging pain . . .

I woke properly and I really did have a pain, an ache like the start of a period across my back and lower stomach. I was bursting for the loo, and it was only when I got out of bed and headed for the bathroom that I realised I was bleeding.

Seventeen

In a Heartbeat

JADE

They totally got the wrong end of the stick, all of them – the ambulance crew, the nurses at the Ledwall hospital and the doctor who examined me. I don't know what Susan said to them, but every last one kept assuring me they were doing all they could to save my baby.

I was woozy with the gas and air they'd given me for the pain, and didn't seem able to string three words together that made any sense. Not that I really knew what to say anyway. That stuff made me sleepy as well. I wished I could just crash out and forget the whole thing. No chance of that though. They were poking and prodding and talking, and putting cold instruments on my belly. Susan was sitting by the bed, more composed and not crying; she must have got someone to look after the boys. I wondered if Paul had been dragged out of work again and thought how cheesed off he was going to be if he had. I hoped he wouldn't come in. Susan coped a lot better when he wasn't around; if he was there she kind of went to pieces.

I was finding her being there quite comforting, though. I'd rather have had her than Jasmine. Jasmine would be all immaculate and in control, Susan was just herself, with her hair pulled back in an untidy ponytail and looking as though she was dying to go outside and have a cigarette. She stayed, though, not talking but she gave my hand a squeeze now and then. When I woke from a doze and found her chair empty, I missed her, which surprised me. I knew she'd only gone to the loo or for a cup of tea and a fag, but there was this odd sense of loss. When I woke next time, the chair was occupied again but not by Susan. It was Rebecca sitting there.

I said, woozily, "Becs, what are you doing here?"

She was looking upset, and her eyes were red. "I got David to drive me over." I wondered how on earth they knew I was in hospital; news travels fast in our small town but I didn't think it was that fast. I couldn't believe it was evening already, but it must have been because it was pitch dark outside.

Becs gulped and leaned forward. "How are you feeling?"

I didn't know really. The pain had eased, though I was still stiff and achey, and I must have been asleep for hours. I wanted to ask why Becs had bothered to come, when I was so nasty the other day. I was glad she did though. There was a lot hanging between us, a lot that could be said, but we didn't get a chance, because a nurse came bustling in. She said, in that annoying cheery way that nurses have, "Now dear, if you don't mind, I'm going to have another little listen to the baby's heartbeat, see what's going on."

I wondered what would happen if I said I did mind, that I just wanted to be left alone, but I didn't have the strength to argue. She pulled the curtains round, then put a thing on my tummy. A look of absolute delight crossed her face. "There it is, a heartbeat, loud and clear. Just listen!"

I heard it, a whooshing and then a kind of muffled rapid hammering sound, much faster than my own heartbeat, which was something I hadn't expected at all. "It's about 125 beats to the minute at this stage," explained the nurse. "All perfectly normal. It will accelerate to more, even as high as 170, and then start to slow down again later on. It's good and strong. I think everything's going to be OK. You've got a little fighter in there."

She beamed at me while she drew back the curtains. I didn't know what to say. I looked across at Rebecca and she had tears on her cheeks. She had heard it too. Hearing that heartbeat had shaken us both.

The nurse said, "The doctor might want to send you for an ultrasound scan, just to check on how baby is doing, but as the bleeding has stopped and the heartbeat is strong, I think I'm pretty safe in saying that the scare is over. They will probably want you to stay in overnight, just to keep an eye on you both, but all being well, you should be home tomorrow. Oh, and by the way, your foster mum was worried that you haven't eaten all day. Supper's over, but would you like me to see if I can rustle up a sandwich or something? Don't forget you're eating for two now!"

I didn't know whether to laugh or cry. I wasn't in control any more; everything had been taken out of my hands. I couldn't imagine the nurse's face if I told her I was due for a termination later this week. I wasn't sure I wanted to tell her anyway. The sound of that rapid heartbeat had done something to me. My baby wanted to live. It was a fighter, the nurse had said.

I remembered, suddenly, that in spite of everything, my own mother had chosen to give me the chance of life. Did I have the right to take that chance away? I'd been thinking of it as a mass of cells, an inconvenience to be dealt with, but it had a heartbeat. I wanted to tell all this to Becs, to tell her she was right, to see that wonderful smile of hers instead of tears, but the nurse was waiting for an answer. "Will ham or cheese be OK for sandwiches?" she asked. "And nice big mug of hot chocolate?"

My mind was whirling, trying to make sense of all that had happened and what it meant, but I managed to answer. "Yes, please. I'm really hungry now."

Eighteen

Panic

REBECCA

Monday was rather a weepy day altogether as it turned out, but it certainly ended up better than I could have hoped.

I'd dreaded going into school more than I'd ever dreaded anything before. It would be all round school that I was pregnant. Deny it all I liked, I'd have a hard job convincing anyone. And Adam and I had almost crossed the line into dangerous territory, the line we'd agreed not to cross, with never a thought for the consequences. It would have been so easy and seemed so right. I hadn't seen him over the weekend, and he hadn't even called or texted, so I didn't know if anything had changed between us. I'd wanted to go further as much as he had. I'd led him on. What if he didn't respect me any more?

And then Jade got up and spilled the beans in

front of the whole class. I knew she'd done it for me. I knew it would mean a whole lot more hassle for her. I didn't know if we were still speaking, but I made up my mind there and then that I'd make the first move if need be.

But then I couldn't because she disappeared from school. Suzie and Kelly and Siobhan were all agog, questioning me. Had I known about all this? Who was the dad? Serve her right, the stuck-up cow. She'd probably get expelled, and good riddance.

And then Lucy, who lived in Jade's street and was home from school ill, texted Siobhan and said that Jade had been rushed to hospital in an ambulance. The goss spread like wildfire about that, too. She'd tried to get rid of the baby herself. She'd tried to commit suicide. I couldn't stand it any longer. I told Mr Phelps I was feeling ill myself and got permission to go home.

Mum was there, between work shifts, and was surprised to see me. I couldn't keep any pretence going with Mum, she'd see straight through me. So I told her everything, or almost everything, over a cup of tea at the kitchen table.

"Well," she said, "I must say I'm not entirely surprised about all of this." I stared at her. I hadn't mentioned the dad, or the circumstances. Mum probably assumed it was a boy our age. "Poor girl," she said. "I could see she was vulnerable under all that confident stuff. You say she's gone to hospital?"

"Yes, and I'm really worried, Mum. I wish I could go and see her, and find out what's going on."

Mum reached across the table and squeezed my hand. "I understand that, love. You're a good friend. I'd take you myself, but my next shift starts soon. You could try phoning the hospital though?"

I tried, but they wouldn't give me any information because I wasn't a relative. I tried Jade's mobile, but it was switched off. I tried the land line at her foster parents' and got the answerphone. Then David came in from college. No point in keeping the story from him, it would be all round town by now. One thing about David, he does listen. And another thing, he had just passed his driving test and had a car. "I'll take you," he said.

I saw that Mum didn't think much of this idea. The two of us racing to the hospital would not appeal to her. But, to give her her due, she didn't say we couldn't, just to drive very carefully and please, please, not to exceed the speed limit.

Anyway, we got to Ledwall hospital safe and sound. I jumped out and rushed inside, leaving David to get the car parked. Inside, I scanned the signs for what might be the right department. I realised I hadn't a clue. And then I saw Jade's foster mother, Susan, coming from the toilet area. She was looking frazzled.

"How is she?" I asked.

"OK – I think. She's had a threatened miscarriage, but the bleeding's just about stopped and she's very sleepy now."

I was so relieved that everything was going to be OK that I smiled.

Susan didn't smile back though. She looked at me, her brows drawn together in a frown. "Did you know she was pregnant, Rebecca?"

I nodded. No use denying it. I thought she'd be mad at me because I knew and she didn't. But she just looked kind of sad. "Poor girl. I wish I'd known."

"I know, I'm sorry." I paused. "Will they let me see her?"

"I don't see why not. She's in a room on her own, and it must be about visiting time now anyway. She's asleep at the moment. To be honest, I could do with a break. I'm gasping for a cup of tea and I need to ring Paul and sort something out for picking up the boys."

She pointed me in the right direction. Jade was asleep, her hair fanned out on the pillow. I sat quietly in the chair next to the bed and waited for her to wake, and I even cried a little. It all seemed so sad.

And then she woke, and we were wondering what to say to each other, and the nurse came in, and we all heard that heartbeat. At that moment something seemed to change in Jade; it was as though a mask had dropped and there was a kind of softness that wasn't there before. I started crying again, while the nurse waffled on about scans and sandwich fillings, and Jade said she was hungry, but I could see that she wanted the nurse to go so that she could cry herself. And she did, with big gasping sobs, and she couldn't seem to say anything, but I sat on the bed and held her and she clung on to me, and we were both shedding so many tears that the hospital sheet was soon soaked through. And I had this feeling of certainty that somehow, in spite of all the difficulties and hard times that might be ahead, everything was going to be all right.

PART TWO

A New Start

Nineteen

Looking Forward to Normal

JADE

I was back at the hospital again, but this time it wasn't a mad dash to A&E; it was a planned ante-natal clinic appointment. Today was the day for my anomaly scan. I was nearly nineteen weeks pregnant.

In the last few weeks, since that first trip to hospital, so much had changed. The morning sickness had passed, and the general tired feeling along with it. A whole new school term had passed, and I'd survived.

Rebecca came to the scan with me. It was a warm, sunny April day, and daffodils were tossing their heads in the beds outside the hospital. It was the Easter holidays, so neither of us were missing anything at school.

"Did Susan mind you not asking her to come this

time?" Rebecca asked when I first mentioned the appointment.

"She didn't say. I think she was cool with it." To be honest, I think Susan was a bit put out. She'd come for the twelve week scan with me, and got quite excited about it. She'd peered at the picture on the screen for ages, working out which bit of the baby was which. All I could see was this dark, grainy, black and white shape which didn't look like anything much to me. I didn't even want a photo, but I took one for Susan's sake. It made me shudder a bit, to be honest, and I certainly wouldn't be showing it all round school or putting it on Facebook. I put it at the bottom of a drawer in my bedroom, under some school text books.

I had to try hard to keep this pregnancy from interfering too much with my life, what with the growing bump and medical appointments. I knew it couldn't be helped for several months, but after that, all would be normal again and I was definitely looking forward to that.

I shifted uncomfortably on the seat. I'd been told I needed a full bladder for this scan, and I was thinking that's a lot to ask. Appointments are never on time, there are other people waiting for scans, presumably all with full bladders. Recipe for disaster, if you ask me. Could even end in floods in the waiting room.

Rebecca looked at me anxiously. "Are you OK?" She was turning into a right mother hen.

"Couldn't be better," I told her. To be honest, I was feeling rather good, apart from the pressing need for the toilet. I had plenty of energy, my skin was clear and my hair shiny. A nurse told me that the second trimester is a good time. The three trimesters are known as weary, cheery and dreary, she said.

I had the beginnings of a little bump, but not too much yet. My clothes still fitted OK and I could even wear my normal jeans, though sometimes I had to lie down on the bed to zip them up. I was wearing stretchy leggings more often – I did that day; tight jeans cutting in would have been the final straw.

I just couldn't wait for September to come. Five more months, exams to take, the summer holidays to get through, a couple of weeks of school and then it would all be over. Back to normal. With luck, I'd be back to school as fast as possible and get quickly back on track for the final year.

"Are you sure adoption is what you want?" Susan had asked me, when the dust had settled after the miscarriage scare.

"Positive," I said firmly. "Makes sense, doesn't it? Families adopting babies are usually loaded, they can give kids everything. They have nice houses and holidays abroad and stuff. I can't do that, not yet."

"You'd be its mum though," she said, but I shook my head and said I wasn't ready to be anyone's mum.

I meant that too, thinking of my own mum. She hadn't been ready and she couldn't hack it. I wasn't going to go down that road.

I thought Susan looked relieved but a bit sad as well. Did she think she'd have to cope with me and the baby if I kept it? She'd already said I could stay with her and Paul, afterwards, if I wanted, and that was cool with me. But a baby too – maybe just too much for her to get her head around.

A few weeks ago, Susan had called me into her bedroom because she wanted to show me something. She pulled open a drawer in her fitted unit, and then another. Piles of little baby clothes; sleep suits, little hats and gloves, tops, even a fluffy hooded all-in-one. I looked at her in amazement. "What's all this?"

"The reason I'm fostering, really," she said, stroking a soft little yellow cardigan and looking sad. "We wanted kids, Paul and me. I was pregnant, seven times, seven pregnancies, seven miscarriages. I can't carry a baby to term. So we had to accept it. I'd have adopted, but Paul wasn't keen. And I couldn't have coped with fostering little babies and then giving them up. So we decided on older kids. Mind, the boys turned out more of a handful than we expected. But they're good kids. You're the first teenager we've taken on."

And I bet you've regretted it once or twice, I thought,

but I didn't say anything. There was turning out to be a lot more to Susan than met the eye. Not only was she willing to keep me on, but she'd been kind in all sorts of ways that surprised me.

She put the little clothes carefully away and closed the drawer. "I just couldn't bear to throw anything away. Paul thinks I'm nuts. Anyway, I just thought – if you were keeping the baby – all these things would be ready and waiting."

"Nice thought," I said. She really did seem a bit nuts, but I was surprised to find I really did want to make her feel better. Those little clothes had made me feel a bit weird, waiting there with no baby to wear them. "Maybe it could take a few things with it, to start it off kind of thing." That actually seemed to brighten her up. Poor Susan. I almost wished I could let her adopt my baby, but I wanted to stay here myself, so that wouldn't work.

I really hated all this waiting about, even if I didn't desperately need to pee. All those pregnant mums, going on about their symptoms and their swollen veins and their husbands and their other kids. Even the younger ones were wittering on about travel systems and child minders and what their mums say and how they'd been decorating their babies' rooms. Some had their partners with them. Some of the mums had been giving me dirty looks because their blokes were looking at me instead of paying attention to them. Well, that was their tough luck. They needn't think I was enjoying it.

I sighed and changed position again.

"You OK?" Rebecca asked for the umpteenth time and I wanted to yell no I'm not, but just nodded. No use moaning and complaining. She grinned and said, "I was just going to ask if I should get you a cup of tea, but maybe not."

"Bad idea," I groaned, and crossed my legs again. I had to say Becs was handling this a lot better than she did that first time. No passing out on the floor for her today. She had a whole lot more confidence about her altogether. Whether it was the relationship with Adam or something else, I didn't know, but she had a kind of glow about her and seemed to be getting prettier all the time. I was glad I got her to have her hair bobbed, it really suited her.

I was just having a check to see how her nails were doing when it was my turn to go in.

Twenty

The Scan

REBECCA

I really hadn't a clue what an anomaly scan was when Jade told me that's what she was having, so I looked it up online. Turns out it's something they do at eighteen to twenty-one weeks, to look at the baby's heart, brain, spinal cord, face, kidneys and abdomen, and check for a dozen or so conditions it might have. When I saw that, it got me a bit worried. If the baby has some of those conditions you can opt for a termination, and I couldn't face that again, not after all that happened before.

"Anyone would think you're the one having it," said Jade when I mentioned all this. I did feel like I had a personal interest in this baby, like I was a kind of extra parent or something. So I did what I do whenever in doubt, went to Mary and asked her to pray about it. She was always so understanding, and often discreetly enquired about my friend and how she was doing. I felt that between us we were helping Jade along since she made the brave decision to have the baby.

"So she's about half way along now," said Mary, when I got a moment alone with her after Cellar Club. I hadn't worked that out for myself and was rather amazed. Everyone had gone home except Adam, who was clearing up in the kitchen. I explained to Mary my worries about the scan.

"So please could you pray that everything will be fine?" I asked. She smiled and leaned forward a little. She looked a little tired. Supervising teenage kids on a regular basis could not be easy on top of all her other vicar's wife duties.

"Yes, I can pray, but I'm going to suggest that you pray too, Rebecca. It's not all down to me, you know."

I was a little taken aback. "But, but you're the vicar's wife. I'm just an ordinary person."

She patted my knee gently. "Listen, Rebecca, your prayers are every bit as important as those of a vicar's wife, or a vicar, or a bishop, or the Archbishop of Canterbury! Never forget that. God listens to *everyone's* prayers. And your concern for your friend is from the heart. That's what counts."

"Well, OK. I'll try. But I might get it wrong."

"You won't. You can't. Because it says in the Bible

that Jesus himself takes our prayers and presents them perfect before his Father God. Just try."

So I did. I prayed in just ordinary words, right there and then, like Mary does: "Dear God, please let Jade's baby be all right when she goes for the scan." Or something like that. And then I added *thank you* because it seemed more polite.

"There, you did it. And now I'll pray too, because two people agreeing in prayer is a powerful thing." When she'd finished praying, she was thoughtful for a moment, and then she said, "Rebecca, would you like Jesus to be in your life?"

I was a bit surprised. I supposed she meant like he was in hers, and the vicar's. I wasn't sure I wanted to be as religious as that, but before I could think of a polite answer there was a loud crash from the kitchen area, and Adam's voice saying "Uh-oh! Mum, we're two mugs less now. Soz! Have you got a brush and dustpan?"

There was no more private conversation that evening as we all helped to clear up the mess.

I looked at Jade's tummy as the woman spread gel across it. It was definitely not as flat as it used to be. She'd been moaning about the added inches and looking for stretch marks already, but she was going to get a lot bigger than this. There was another person in there, growing every day. We heard the heartbeat again, fast and regular.

And then the technician was moving the scanner thing over Jade's tummy and a picture was coming up on the screen. I couldn't make any sense of the fuzziness to begin with, but suddenly it took shape and I could make out a lighter shape inside a dark cavity, that was kind of curled around but definitely had a human form. A baby! I felt my eyes grow round as the scan focused on different areas; arms with hands and fingers, raised up towards the face and clasped together, legs that were curled up towards the round little tummy with toes on the feet. I saw a face in profile, a face with ears, closed eyes, a little snub nose and a mouth. It was a real baby!

I looked at Jade. She was watching the screen picture too, with a strange expression on her face. When she saw me looking, she turned her eyes away. But we had both seen the same thing. One of the little legs suddenly gave a kick, and one of the hands fluttered about in front of the face.

"Look, he – or she – is waving to you!" the woman exclaimed. She explained it was not in a position where we could tell if it was a boy or a girl, but as she did all the measurements and checked the organs, she told us it looked healthy, active and the right size for its dates. It was already twelve centimetres long, was well nourished and just as it should be. Our prayers had worked!

I was totally bowled over. This was like the babies we saw on Mary's film, but this time it was real . . . Jade's baby . . . and in another five months or less it would be out in the world and we'd get to meet it!

Except maybe we wouldn't. While the technician went on explaining all the things that were happening right now, waffling on about the baby swallowing amniotic fluid and weeing it out again, and that babies sometimes play with the umbilical cord because they like to use their hands, I found my mind wandering, although my eyes were still fixed on that little blurry picture on the screen. How soon do they take babies away if they're being adopted?

I stole another look at Jade, but she had closed her eyes. Maybe she was trying not to think about the little figure on the screen, and focus on her life plan. I wondered if she would be able to hold her baby, cuddle it before it goes. Would she give it a name? Would she be allowed to know where it lived, or write to it or be in touch at all? She had told me she didn't want to do any of those things, but how could she bear not to? I couldn't if it was me. But then she's Jade, a law unto herself.

I turned back to the screen, but not before I saw one small tear escape from a closed eye and trickle down Jade's cheek.

Twenty-one

Easter Sunday

REBECCA

Adam and I were in a place we both love – the biggest bookshop in Ledwall. Both of us had notebooks in our hands because we were here on serious business. The bookshelves at the Cellar Club were finished, and waiting to be stocked. There had been some debate about how effective this would be. Adam had his doubts. Although he loved books, he and most other people our age spent more time reading and researching electronically than from the pages of a print book.

"Tables with computers, like they have in libraries, might work better than books on shelves," he said. "Not everybody has a laptop or a tablet of their own."

We'd talked about this, having dinner at the vicarage with his mum and dad. I'd discovered that Adam's dad is the bookish one, Mary is definitely more a people person.

"I'm not sure," she said doubtfully. "Think of the expense. The church council aren't going to fork out big sums of money for electronic equipment, even if they had the funds to spare. They're stretched as it is, and a couple of them don't approve of the Cellar Club; they think church funds could be put to better use. I think a good selection of books, preferably second hand, would go down a lot better. Don't you think so, dear?" she appealed to her husband.

The vicar is a man after my own heart. He nodded. "I prefer a good book myself, always have. And you're right about the church council. Expensive technical stuff for teenagers would be way down on their agenda."

I had to agree. I did stuff online as much as anybody, and e-readers are great in their way, but there's nothing like a real printed book in your hands, with paper pages to turn instead of flicking a button, and the book there to refer to any time you want to, in my opinion.

The great thing was, I could give my opinion here, and they listened. They weighed it up and talked it through. It had helped a lot with my confidence. I loved being there, and I was growing increasingly fond of Adam's parents, who I thought of as Mary and The Vicar. Not that it was always peaceful and quiet; sometimes there were other people sharing a meal, usually old people, or someone who was in some kind of trouble, or even a homeless person. I liked the bustle and variety, and I liked it that Adam and I were expected to help with preparing and serving the food and cleaning up afterwards, especially if there was a moment for a bit of snogging over the soapsuds. And I liked the talk round the table.

This particular discussion ended when someone remembered that the cellar was a poor place for electronic devices, with hardly any reception. So there we were, checking out books. Mostly fiction, but some biographies and books for stuff like photography. Not that we were going to buy new copies, we were being cheeky and checking out the best sellers among young people. There was a secondhand section upstairs, and in the end we came away with a good haul, plus ideas that we could follow up later online. We felt we'd earned a latte in the little coffee shop next door.

It had only been a few days since my visit to the hospital with Jade, and seeing her baby on the scan. It had been on my mind ever since. Her baby was perfect, just as Mary and I prayed it would be. Did God do that, or would it have just been the same anyway? I couldn't forget what she said about having Jesus in my life either. What did she mean? How did that work?

I looked at Adam across the table. He was so gorgeous, with his hair all rumpled because he runs his hands through it when he's trying to decide things.

He has nice hands, square and practical, and his mother's deeply searching eyes. I remembered the way his hands felt that evening in the vicarage, how it felt to bury my own hands in his hair . . .

I lowered my eyes. That kind of thinking was dangerous, and we'd made a new pact, not to spend too much time alone together in each other's homes, or anywhere else for that matter, until after exams. But it was hard.

I dragged myself back from those kind of thoughts. Adam was flicking through the pages of one of the new books. He closed it and put it back in the bag.

"What are you thinking?"

Back in the day I would have blushed like mad and I was pleased with myself because I didn't. I really was less shy these days. All the same, I was not admitting to those kinds of thoughts in the middle of a busy mall crowded with Easter shoppers. I remembered what was on my mind before. "I was just wondering what your mum meant the other night, when she asked me if I'd like Jesus in my life."

He grinned and rolled his eyes. "Mum thinks everyone should have Jesus in their lives. Dad too, but he's not so up front about it in conversation. He preaches about it all the time though. Why, does it bother you?"

"No, I don't think so," I said slowly, "but I'd like to know what she meant."

He downed the last of his coffee. "Well, why don't you come to church on Sunday? It's Easter, they make a big thing of it."

"Could I? Could I sit with you?"

He grinned again. "I might let you, if you play your cards right."

Easter fell late that year, and the daffodils and primroses were out everywhere with their bright splashes of colour. The grass between the gravestones in the churchyard had been newly mown, and had that wonderful fresh grass smell. I'd never been in the main church building before. It was dim and cool in the porch, but inside sunlight was shining through the stained glass windows, sending bright colours across the tiled floor. I'd expected straight-backed wooden pews, but there were rows of comfortable light beech framed chairs with blue padded seats and backs. The ones on the ends of the rows even had arms.

"Dad and Mum got the pews thrown out," said Adam as we found seats. "They said you couldn't expect people to come to church if the seats did their backs in. A lot of the old fogies made a fuss about it. They hate change."

I'd wondered if Adam would wear a suit for church. He didn't; just a denim jacket and jeans, but he looked nice. I had a new top and cardigan with my black trousers and felt I fitted in. Some of the people here were dressed up, some even had hats, but lots were just dressed casually. There were lots of people and the place was buzzing with conversation.

Mary was there, sitting in the front row in a floral skirt and pink jacket. She turned and waved and smiled at the two of us. I had quite a shock when the music changed and Adam's dad came down the aisle and went up the steps to the little platform place. I'd never seen him in anything but old corduroys and a checked shirt or jumper, always a bit rumpled and with glasses on the end of his nose. He seemed a different person, in a long black robe with an embroidered white one over it and a long gold scarf-thing around his neck.

A hush fell as he turned and looked out over the congregation. I expected some kind of long speech to begin with, but he just raised his arms and said "Christ is risen!" and to my surprise, all the audience responded with a kind of loud chant that almost raised the roof: "He is risen indeed!"

And then we sang this song called "Christ the Lord is Risen Today!" and everyone's voices sounded like a kind of massive celebration and there was this feeling of joy. I looked round and saw the same happiness in people's faces, and I knew that there was something special here among them, and whatever it was, I wanted it too.

Twenty-two

Faith

REBECCA

When I look back, that Easter Sunday was a real turning point for me. For me and Adam. I'd not been to many church services before; weddings and my great-gran's funeral when I was little, but never one like that. It was so different to what I'd imagined.

When we did the prayers, listened to the readings from the Bible and sang the hymns, there was this sense of joy, of triumph, of everything turning out all right. And when the vicar got up to do the talk, I was spellbound.

I'd heard of Jesus, of course, but always thought he was just one of the goodies from history. Now I was hearing that he was much more than that, that he was the Son of God come to earth as a baby (at Christmas), to live in the humblest way as a man and then eventually to die in place of all the evil in the world, all the bad that's inside everyone (it's called sin). But he didn't stay dead, he rose to life again at Easter, and in doing so made it possible for everyone who believes in him to live for ever.

I believed it. I knew it was true, because I saw what made Adam's parents the people they are; Jesus was living in them and loving other people through them. I suddenly understood why Mary had asked if I wanted Jesus in *my* life.

I did want it, I wanted it so badly that I could hardly speak a coherent word as the service ended. Everyone was greeting everyone else, they were hugging and kissing and smiling and laughing, full of happiness that it was Easter, and that Jesus had defeated evil and brought a new life to all who wanted it. I made a beeline for the vicar as he headed for the door to greet everyone as they left.

Adam came after me as I pushed my way through the mass of people. "Hey, wait for me! What's the hurry?"

I was still having difficulty speaking. All I could say, breathlessly, was "I want it!" I squeezed between two rather large ladies and got to the vicar as he reached the porch, actually grabbing his long white robe. He felt the tug, and turned, surprised.

"Rebecca?"

"I want it!" was still all I could manage to say. I

could see at once he understood perfectly. He didn't ask a single thing, just smiled this big smile so I could see the love shining out of his eyes, and reached out his hand to me and said, "Praise God!" People were backing up around us waiting to shake his hand, so he added, "Rebecca, can you get to the vicarage in half an hour or so? I'm going to be busy here for a little while, but either Mary or I will get back there just as soon as we can."

I nodded and thanked him and said I could. Mum was making an Easter Sunday roast, but there was still plenty of time.

It was actually Mary who sat with me in the vicarage study a bit later, while the vicar, without his robes and wearing a large striped apron, clattered about in the kitchen with Adam. Every time the door opened, a lovely smell of roasting lamb drifted in. Mary listened to me, and explained more about Jesus, and answered my questions as though she had all the time in the world and I was the only person who mattered. And then we prayed together, and I felt as though everything had become new, and I understood the phrase that I'd heard somewhere – "born again".

I left there feeling as though I was walking on air. Mary had said I was welcome to stay for lunch, but I'd promised Mum I'd be home. Adam said he'd text me later, with what I felt was rather a quizzical look.

I tried hard to explain to him what had happened when we met again that evening. I couldn't stop smiling. We'd gone for a walk down by the river. He knew all the terminology much better than I did, having listened to his dad's sermons week after week. But I could see there were things that puzzled him.

"It's like I always say – how can you prove all this about God and Jesus and the Bible? I mean, I believe it's real for you. I can see how happy you are, that you really believe it and all that. But how did you *prove* it was real before you decided?"

"I didn't," I said. "And I can't, not in the way you mean. But I don't think anyone can. You have to just make up your mind you're going to believe it." I had a sudden flash of inspiration. "You remember that scene in *Indiana Jones and the Last Crusade?* Where his instructions tell him to step off the cliff into thin air? He makes the decision to obey and steps out. Only he doesn't fall, because there's that rock bridge going across the chasm, only he couldn't see it from where he was standing before. He had to step out in faith because that's what the instructions said. Get it?"

"Er – I think so. You just have to make a decision, doubts and all, and act on it?"

"Exactly."

"But what if there wasn't a bridge, what if it doesn't work? Won't that prove it's all a big con?"

"Is that what you reckon your mum and dad are, con artists?"

"Well, no, of course not!" He gave me a dig in the ribs. "They mean it all right. But maybe it doesn't work for everyone. What about Buddhists and Hindus and sun worshippers and Muslims and all the other things people believe? They all think they're right too!"

I sighed. I didn't have any answers. There were so many things I still wanted to ask, myself. I said, "Your mum and dad are running a course for people who want to know what Christianity's all about, starting next week. I've said I'll go. Why don't you come as well?"

He rolled up his eyes and sighed. "I've heard it all before, but anything for a quiet life. OK."

When I got home I made a new resolution. I'd write a journal, a brand new one, and keep it up regularly. Because today was the first day of my new life.

Twenty-three

Doubt and Faith

REBECCA

I didn't really know what had happened, but something definitely had. It was as though I'd been made over new, like when you have a brand new book to read and turn to the first page, all clean and fresh and pristine. And Mary said you can make a new start every time you do something wrong, if you tell God you're sorry. Not like books, that get grubbier as you read them and get finger marks and scuffs and smears from chocolate and jam if you like to munch when you're reading, like me.

The group for new Christians and people interested in learning about it started the week after Easter. Another couple who'd just got married came, John and Olivia – they were really nice. Adam came with me to the first meeting, so there were the six of us, with the vicar and Mary. I thought Adam must have known everything about the Bible from listening to his dad, but he was still trying to prove things, before he'd believe them for himself. He had a logical mind and wanted hard evidence. John was the same; maybe it's a bloke thing. Adam said it was easy for me to believe anything because I have a wild imagination. I didn't know whether that was a compliment or not. John said the same thing about Olivia and we all laughed about it.

We didn't fall out over it, though. In fact, Adam told me afterwards it's made me a more interesting person and he liked me having my own opinions. Not that I wasn't interesting before, he quickly added – I told him he'd better stop before he dug himself into a big hole!

School came round too quick after the holidays. I hardly saw Jade over Easter, apart from a couple of revision sessions, and I felt a bit bad about it. She and Susan and Paul and the boys went off to a holiday camp for a few days, so that was a nice change for her hopefully, although holiday camps aren't her thing. She'd been quiet since she had the last scan. I didn't really know what she was thinking and she didn't want to talk about it.

She was definitely getting bigger. Since we saw the scan picture I couldn't stop thinking about that little person she was carrying around with her. It was real! Or rather, it was not an "it" but a "he" or "she"! Sad to think I might never see him or her. I know this sounds weird, because it wasn't my baby, but I kind of loved it already, and I wondered if Jade was trying not to. I wished I could do something to help. Well, I could always pray, and I did.

At the second meeting of the Christian group, Olivia asked how, if God is real, he can allow such terrible suffering in the world. I'd been wondering that myself. You only have to look at all the refugees living in terrible conditions, and the horrific terrorist attacks, and all the other dreadful things.

I can't remember the vicar's reply exactly, but we had a really interesting discussion about having the freedom to choose right or wrong, and sin in the world, and so often how we choose hatred and pride and revenge and greed and all sorts of bad stuff, instead of following God's way, which is love and peace and kindness, and the devil putting fear and lies into people's hearts, because he's the biggest liar of all.

I was learning so much it was hard to take it all in, and I hadn't realised the devil was real. Mary gave us all a Bible, and showed us where to start reading – in the Gospels, because they tell the story of Jesus.

So I started reading every day, last thing at night, in bed, before writing about it in my journal. Reading about Jesus just blew my mind – sometimes it was midnight before I turned off my lamp! He was God, and yet he was so human, so full of joy, so loving and caring and gentle, but he didn't mind telling horrid people exactly what was coming to them. I felt like I'd fallen in love with him, though in a totally different way to the way I loved Adam, of course.

The next Saturday, Jade phoned and asked if I'd go shopping with her in Ledwall. "I just have to get some new clothes. I'm not kidding you, mine are all held together with safety pins. I can't get into any of my jeans, even the stretchy ones . . ."

I thought she still looked fabulous – we're talking about Jade here – and I told her so, but I knew she didn't believe a word of it. She was convinced she looked like an elephant already.

We got the bus into Ledwall and hit the shops, stocking up with leggings and loose tops, and shirts, and some bigger size underwear.

"Would you be interested in nursing bras?" asked the lady in the lingerie department, sussing out Jade's bump. Jade and I looked at each other, puzzled. I could see she didn't know what those were, and neither did I. Something nurses wore? The lady took pity on us. "I'll show you some," she said, and fetched out some dreadful sturdy-looking things with flaps to let down for breast feeding.

We looked at each other again, hardly knowing what to think. "Er - I don't think so, thank you." Jade managed to say, and when we got out of the shop we had a fit of the giggles and she said, "Imagine wearing something as disgusting as that! As if!" It was good to see her having a laugh.

I'd been meaning to tell Jade about becoming a Christian, and today seemed as good as any, so when we stopped for a drink in a café later I did tell her. She looked at me as though I'd totally flipped.

"I thought everyone was a Christian in this country, except if they're Muslim or Hindu or something," she said.

"No, it's something you have to decide for yourself," I told her.

She stirred her tea and rolled up her eyes. "OK, whatever, if it makes you happy. I don't somehow think it would suit me though."

The following Thursday, I debated with myself whether I should skip the Christian group and get on with revision. Everyone was cramming like mad, with exams just round the corner. But I decided I wasn't going to miss the group for anything.

That evening, John said he wanted to believe in God, but couldn't because he had so many doubts and questions. Like, what if it's all a made-up story? And if it's true, how can God possibly know every single person who's ever lived, let alone love them? How can he love people when some are so awful? Nice people, yes. But what about people who abuse children, and murderers? Can God really forgive them?

I felt Adam prick up his ears, because those are the kinds of things he says. Mary and the vicar were away that day at some kind of conference, and Paul was leading, a young colleague of Adam's dad I think. He said that even the most awful sins can be forgiven. And that it's OK to have doubts and questions and things we can't understand. God is so big he can't be understood. If we did, he'd be no different to us. Adam chatted to him so long afterwards that I ended up going home on my own.

The next day after school, Adam came round to my house and told me he had something to tell me, but we had to go out. Intrigued, I got my jacket and we went down to our favourite spot by the river. He was fairly bursting with the news. "After you went home last night, I stayed talking to Paul for ages. I don't really know how it happened, but as we were talking, I could suddenly see what was meant by taking a step of faith. You just have to DO it, doubts and all! So I did."

I stopped in my tracks. "Adam! Really? You really did?"

He nodded. "I really did. Stepped out on that invisible bridge like you said. Paul prayed with me, and said not to worry about all the questions and doubts – and I still have plenty, by the way – but just to take the first step."

I hugged him. "Your mum and dad are gonna be so pleased!"

Later, I recorded the day as a RED LETTER day in my journal.

Twenty-four

A Nasty Shock

JADE

It was no fun being pregnant. Actually, I hated it. Especially when sitting in a hot classroom. Especially in a heat wave . . . but there was one day which stood out as worse than all the others.

It was late June and the hottest day of the year so far. It was unbearable for everyone, although I was the only one who was pregnant. There was a ceiling fan that was supposed to cool things down in the English classroom, but didn't do anything much, apart from make an irritating clicking sound.

I so badly wanted to concentrate. I needed to get good grades; my future life depended on it, but the heat zapped away every last bit of energy I still had. Even when our shirts were sticking to our backs we weren't allowed to have the windows open, because of the high pollen count, apparently, although I suspect

Suzie was only making a fuss about her allergies to get attention.

I was into the last trimester of pregnancy, the bit the midwife called "dreary" and she wasn't wrong. The bump was huge now and I'd had to get new black trousers with elasticated waist (yuck) and a size bigger in school shirts, which I wore outside the trousers. I couldn't help contrasting my current image with the way I'd made my entrance into the form room that first morning and everyone's eyes had almost popped out. Now I had to be the ugliest girl in the class. Swap good legs and cleavage for swollen ankles, massive boobs and heartburn if I wasn't careful what I ate. Sigh.

School chairs didn't help, either – they have to be the worst ever, and I was forever shifting about trying to make myself comfortable, which was pretty much impossible. The baby kicked about at the most inconvenient times. I wished it would just go to sleep. It always seemed at its most lively when I wanted to sleep myself, or concentrate on studying, or just forget about it all for a bit. When it first started to move I didn't know what it was. No mistaking it now though.

Anyway, this worst day ever, I sat in that English class, trying to get my head round the relationship between Lennie and George in *Of Mice and Men*. My mind wandered to my last meeting with Jasmine. We'd gone through all the options I had for the baby, not that I wanted to hear them, but she was insistent.

"You have to be clear in your mind when you're making decisions like this," she had said. Termination ("killing" as Becs put it) was no longer an option, so we'd talked about adoption in more depth. Jasmine even asked me if there was any chance I felt I could keep the baby. "A lot of girls do," she said. "Mind you, some do it for all the wrong reasons. They think a baby will love them unconditionally, that it will be a little cuddly thing to dress up and show off, but there's not much love going round when you've had a sleepless night for the umpteenth time and there are still nappies to change and feeds to make. A child doesn't give back much for a while. It's pretty tough for a young mum on her own. Some do make it though. Have you really considered this as one of your choices?"

I'd given her a firm NO. Not that she knew anything about pregnancy or having a baby – she'd never had one. Keeping this baby was definitely not part of the plan, though, for any reason. I just wanted it to go away so I could get my life back. Ten weeks and counting.

I remember looking across at Rebecca. She was frowning and biting her lip, scribbling away as though her life depended on it. English is her fave subject, and relationships her speciality. Her bobbed hair swung across her face and she brushed it back. Then she looked up and caught my eye, and smiled, and the whole situation seemed lighter somehow. She had that effect. Frankly, if I hadn't had Rebecca as a friend I don't know what I'd have done.

Her glance slid across to where Adam was sitting and her smile became what you could only describe as radiant as he returned her gaze. They had a kind of unspoken telepathy, those two. They were soul mates. I doubted I'd ever have someone in my life like that. It never used to bother me but now sometimes it did. A little. It must be nice to have that kind of relationship. Exactly the opposite of what I'd had with Henry.

It was a relief all round when the buzzer went and class was over. The rest of the day was free. "Going to put your feet up now, Jade? We're going swimming," said Kelly with false sweetness, and she and Siobhan had a little snigger. I really couldn't be bothered with them. I guessed Rebecca and Adam would be going swimming with some of the others. I'd have liked a swim myself, but I felt humongous in a swimsuit and a perfect target for more bitchiness, so I started to head for home. Then I heard Rebecca calling.

"Hang on Jade, wait for me, shall I come round yours? We could finish the essay together?"

"Aren't you going swimming with Adam?"

"No, he's got a driving lesson this afternoon. Takes his test in three weeks! Bet he'll pass first time too."

I bet he would. And when he got wheels, I'd see even less of Becs. But, hey ho, September and freedom were not so far away.

Both of us were gasping for a drink by the time we got to my house, so we went to grab something cold from the fridge. Susan and Paul were both out and the boys in school, so the house was quiet. They'd left stuff lying about all over the hall though, as usual. I was shoving a football boot under the hall stand with my foot when I noticed a letter propped up there addressed to me. Strange. Real handwriting, too. Didn't get many of those nowadays. I opened it, started to read, and heard myself gasp. Rebecca looked at me anxiously. "What is it? You've gone pale. Is it bad news?"

"It's from Henry." My legs had gone wobbly and I had to sit down. We went into the kitchen and pulled out a couple of chairs. I read the letter aloud.

"My dear Jade, It seems such an age since I saw you, and I've missed you every single day. I want to explain my situation to you. I expect you will know that I am married. I am sorry I didn't explain fully at the time, but I got rather caught up in events."

I paused in disbelief. "Yeah, like organising a ginormous society wedding." Becs just stared, with her mouth open. I carried on reading.

155

"I want you to realise that this marriage is one of convenience. Our families approved and expected it, and it was a beneficial strategy for all concerned. You'll understand about that. You are the one who captured my heart from the moment I met you, so young, so beautiful, so ambitious. You are forever in my heart. This summer, I shall again be at the Ledwall property while my parents are away. My wife will not be with me for more than a week or two, as she plans to spend most of the summer with her sister in the Caribbean. I would so love to see you again, to take up where we left off, to renew the special bond we had. Please reply and tell me you have not forgotten me.

With sincere love,

Henry C."

Both of us were speechless when I'd finished reading.

"The nerve of it!" said Rebecca at last, her eyes like saucers. "Thinking you'll come running, just like that, even though he's married to someone else!"

"Something to amuse him in dull old Ledwall over the summer," I said, hearing the bitterness in my voice. "Marriage of convenience! The two-timing rat! It would serve him right if I did turn up, bump and all, and say,

"How lovely to see you, dahling! Oh, and by the way, congratulations, you're going to be a daddy soon!"

"Do you think you should tell him?" asked Rebecca. "Or tell his wife?"

I shook my head. I'd already thought that through, long ago. There'd be a huge scandal if this came out. Headlines in the papers and plenty of publicity, but not the sort I wanted. I could demand money. Fathers are legally entitled to support their children – Jasmine had told me that. But I'm not keeping the baby, so I didn't need his money. I just wanted to get September over with as little fuss as possible and get my life back on track again. And as for becoming Henry Chiltern's pet again, no way!

Rebecca was looking at me big-eyed. "What're you going to do?"

"This," I said. I got up and hunted about in a cluttered drawer until I found a box of matches. Then I went over to the sink, struck a match, held it to the letter and watched the paper flare up and turn to black ash. When it was all burned, I turned on the tap and flushed the charred remains down the plughole.

Twenty-five

Bullies

JADE

Hot, hot, hot. I used to love the sunshine and could soak it up for hours; must be the West Indian blood in me. I've always disliked the usual British summer, dreary, drizzly and unpredictable, and normally I'd have been in my element in the heatwave we were having, but not this year. We went to Devon for couple of weeks to stay in a cottage, which wasn't much of a fun journey with two sticky-fingered squabbling kids sharing the back seat with me. (Susan took pity on me on the way home and let me sit in front.) It was a nice break though, even though I did feel like a beached whale. The cottage was tiny, but had a garden with a swing seat, on which I spent most of the week, reading, studying and looking forward to my future life. I planned, of course, to be holidaying in places like the Bahamas in the future.

Apart from that holiday, the summer holidays dragged and I was bored out of my wits. Paul suggested I got a holiday job, but Susan reminded him I was pregnant and there weren't many holiday jobs about where you could sit down. I became more and more irritated with everyone in the household. I spent as much time as I could on the sun lounger in the back garden, with the parasol up, reading fashion mags and trying to remember what it was like before I was the size of a baby whale and could wear a bikini. I didn't get a lot of peace though, except when the boys were off swimming or playing football in the park.

The one thing I looked forward to was going to the swimming pool. Sometimes I went with Becs, sometimes on my own. For obvious reasons I tried to go when it was quiet. Swimming I still enjoyed; the water buoyed up the bump and took the weight, and the cool water was absolute bliss on my skin. I could stay there for hours, just soaking. I really did have stretch marks. Becs said you can hardly see them, just faint lines, but I thought they were hideous. I kept them well plastered with this special cream I found on the internet. I had this grungy maternity swimsuit which did nothing for me but did keep the bump covered. And when I was in the water, it seemed to soothe the baby.

One Friday night I walked to the swimming pool, alone. I did text Becs to see if she wanted to go, but it was her night for going to a church thing with Adam. She always seemed to be going to church these days, I suppose it was because Adam's dad was actually the vicar. She did try to explain it all to me, but I can't say I get excited about religion. Whatever floats your boat, I reckon.

It was quiet in the main pool, hardly anyone about. I went as late as possible to avoid other people. Friday nights are always quiet – I suppose everyone goes down the pub. Paul certainly does. Anyway, I swam up and down, slowly, and then just soaked, letting the water sink into my skin. I didn't care if I came out all wrinkled and waterlogged. It was so relaxing I almost fell asleep.

When I did get out, the water poured off me in streams. I was the last person to leave the pool. The lifeguard must have been itching for me to get out so he could go home. I felt heavy out of the water. Drying my hair and my lumbering body was quite an effort. I pulled on my leggings and T-shirt and slung my bag over my shoulder. Another day almost over, another day nearer freedom.

I heard girls' voices as I made my way home along the short cut from the pool and gym complex to the housing estates. It's a bit of a rough alleyway; Susan had warned me not to go that way, but it had never bothered me before. I'd seen a lot worse in my time. Rounding the corner, I saw it was a group of girls, some from our estate and from the year below me in school. They were smoking and drinking something from cans, something alcoholic by the way they were behaving. Losers. Sadly, I couldn't avoid them, so I just kept walking.

"Well, if it isn't Jiggly Jade," one of them said, and waved a can in my face as I passed. "Have a drink, Jiggly?"

I shook my head and tried to keep walking, but they moved in a group to block my way. "She can't, she's up the duff," said another, which brought on another round of giggling. "Oh yeah, so she is. How could I forget? Pretty obvious really."

She did an imitation of a pregnant woman, belly stuck out and a waddling walk. The others were in stitches. Morons. I made a move to pass but one of them stuck out her arm in front of me. "Not so fast. Tell us what it feels like, being preggers. Who's the daddy, anyway?"

"Let me pass," I said stiffly. I was beginning to get a bit nervous; unusual for me, but those giggling idiots were starting to freak me out. I pushed forward, but the girl with her arm out pushed me back.

"Not so fast, slapper. Naomi asked you a question."

"Who's the daddy?" asked the same girl again, who I suppose was Naomi, and the others took up the chant: "Who's the daddy? Who's the daddy? Who's the daddy?"

I took a step back and bumped into another girl. She gave me a hard shove and I staggered forward again, almost losing my balance. The girls' mood was turning nasty. "Who's the daddy? Tell us, stuck-up slut!"

I told myself I just had to keep my cool and walk away. They'd lose interest if I didn't respond. And then one of them made a comment that cut me to the quick.

"Reject!"

Of course it was probably all round the estate as well as school that I was fostered as well as pregnant. I stopped in my tracks. This was too near the knuckle for me to ignore, touching that hidden place that I guarded like crazy. Because it felt like it was true, and it hurt like mad.

I turned to face the girls and looked at their faces one by one. I would take them all on if I had to. They were staring at me, some grinning, some a bit embarrassed, but all interested to see what I would do next. A little bit of unexpected entertainment to liven up a Friday night.

The one who spoke that word looked pleased to have got a reaction. She said it again, quietly, but loud enough for me to hear. "Reject!" I felt the baby kick hard against my ribs. Could it sense that I was angry? Because I was suddenly so angry that I could hardly think straight. They knew it, and they were waiting to see what I'd do.

And then, suddenly, there were footsteps approaching on the path behind me and a voice, young and male. "What's going on here?"

The tension was broken. The girls dropped their aggressive poses and shuffled their feet. It was a tall young guy, carrying a sports bag, with a towel slung over his shoulder. He'd obviously been working out at the gym. It was Rebecca's brother, David.

"Jade?" he said. "What's going on? Are you getting hassle?"

The girls were looking a bit stupid now. One of them muttered, "We were just having a bit of fun."

"Seemed more like a bit of bullying to me." He was tanned from all the sun we'd been having, and he looked like he'd just showered. He was frowning. "What's more, you're all under-age drinking. I think you'd better all go home."

There was some muttering and funny looks in the group. I could see they were eyeing David and thinking he was a fit guy. They were not wrong there. But they were moving away along the path, and the incident was over.

Normally something like that wouldn't have bothered me, but I suddenly found I was shaking like a leaf. David was looking concerned. Maybe he thought I might be about to go into labour on the spot. "Are you OK?" he asked. "They didn't hurt you, did they?"

I shook my head and started to say, "No, I'm fine," but suddenly reaction set in and I burst into tears. I was annoyed with myself. I never used to be such a wimp.

David didn't turn a hair though. He reached out and put his arm round me and gave me a hug. It was just what I needed and wonderfully comforting. He's very muscular and his arms felt warm and strong and safe. He smelled of shower gel. I'd never had a hug like that from a man before. I leaned into his shoulder.

"There's a seat a bit further along," he said. "Sit down for a bit and you'll feel better. I've got some water in my bag. Been swimming?"

I realised I looked far from my best, with my hair still damp and no make-up. Not to mention the bump. But it didn't seem to matter. He sat with me for a few minutes, not saying anything, and it didn't feel awkward at all.

"I'll walk you home, if you like," he offered when I got up to go, and I thought, yes, that would be good, and thought how kind he was, not to mind walking along with a girl seven months pregnant. He even helped me up off the seat.

"Next time you go swimming," he said, "make sure someone's with you. People use this path going home from the pubs, and you never know. If you let me know, I could meet you after swimming and see you home."

I said, "OK, thanks," and once again it struck me how much like his sister he was when he smiled.

Twenty-six

When Will It Ever End?

JADE

By the middle of August I was just about bored to tears. Bored with the same old place, with getting bigger by the minute, with not being able to wear nice clothes, with heartburn, with swollen ankles, with being unable to get comfortable to sleep, with this other life inside constantly moving and shifting.

"You have a very active baby in there," the midwife had told me at my last ante-natal check. "Always on the go, that one."

"Tell me about it," I'd said gloomily. And it didn't even cheer me up when she told me that everything was looking fine.

"Let's hope all the activity doesn't mean sleepless nights ahead," she said cheerfully, putting away her stethoscope. "That's it. All done now." My regular midwife was on holiday and this one was a stand-in, obviously she didn't know my situation and hadn't read the notes.

Jasmine was all clued up, though. "I'm glad to see you looking so well, Jade," she said on her next visit. She paused. "I thought you might like to know we have a family lined up for – after."

At first I hadn't given a second thought to the adoptive family, but, strangely, I'd been thinking a lot about them lately. I didn't want to meet them, of course, but I'd like to know a bit about them. Jasmine seemed to understand this.

"They're a very nice couple, late thirties, both professional people. She's a GP, he's managing director of an electrical goods company. They have a nice house, several acres of grounds; they are keen on outdoor pursuits. They mentioned something about dogs, and possibly a pony."

For some reason I was focusing on the professional people bit. "Will she be giving up work to look after the baby?"

"Well, I don't know all the details. But I'm sure they'll work it out so that one is there, even if the other has to work. And if they both had to, I imagine they could afford to employ a nanny."

I said quickly, "I don't think nannies are a good idea.

They're being paid to look after a child."

Jasmine looked at me over her glasses. "Well, of course. They're doing a job and they need to be paid for it." She paused. "Jade, you seem to have problems with people in the caring professions and the fact that they're paid for their work. They have to make their livings, you know, like everyone else."

Well, she would say that, wouldn't she, seeing as she was one of them? I wanted to say, yes, but they don't have to pretend to care, do they, when it's just a job? But even in my own mind, that sounded childish. Well, it's how I felt. And although I hadn't had a spat with Jasmine lately, if she wanted one, she could have one.

She leaned forward before I could speak. "Are you having second thoughts, Jade? About the adoption?"

"No way." I would have said more, got a few things off my chest about the caring professions and other things, but just then Susan came in with tea and biscuits and the conversation veered off in another direction. Jasmine and Susan seemed to get on well, surprisingly enough, seeing as they were complete opposites; Jasmine in her smart suits and painted nails, and Susan in her jogging pants and shapeless T-shirts.

Not that I had anything against Susan. Since she had got over the shock of me being pregnant she'd been very supportive, probably far more supportive than some mothers would have been. Not that I would know anything about that. Paul could be an old grouch at times, although it was mainly because I know exactly how to wind him up. But Susan was kind, she even brought me breakfast in bed sometimes at weekends. She cooked me the foods I liked and avoided the ones I didn't. I'd had a terrible craving for kippers with cheese sauce a few weeks before, and she cooked it for me until Paul said the whole house reeked of fish. Thankfully that phase passed, although I still couldn't stand the smell of pesto sauce, it made me heave.

In fact, Susan's attitude mystified me, considering the disappointments over babies she'd had herself. She had difficulty passing a baby clothes shop without going in and buying something. Only the week before she'd bought a little set of baby dungarees and a yellow top and hat to match. Given the piles of baby clothes she had stashed away upstairs, I was beginning to think she had a problem.

Strangely, Becs brought up the same topic about the adoptive parents, later that day when we were walking home together from swimming. Since the evening when I got mobbed by those stupid girls, I'd done what David said and not gone to the pool alone. Usually Becs came. Once or twice I'd texted David and he'd walked home with me. Or rather, he walked and I waddled. Impossible to do anything else these days. I didn't know how he coped with being seen with me, but it didn't seem to bother him. I looked at all the other girls in their shorts and crop tops and tight lycra, and I couldn't believe I'd turned into this humongous, distorted version of what I used to be. I'd had some bad summers before but this had to be the worst ever. I couldn't wait for it to come to an end.

I did enjoy those walks home with David though. He was easy to talk to, and we'd had a few good laughs as well. He was like Becs, but less shy and more outgoing. He was heading for a career in sport after college, he told me, and was keen on sport for disadvantaged kids. One of life's good guys, and cool with it. Once or twice, I'd caught myself thinking it would be nice if he'd give me another hug. Wishful thinking, as if.

So when Becs said, thoughtfully, slowing down to my snail-like pace, "Jade, do you get to meet the – er – adoptive parents?" I was irritated.

"Don't you start as well! I've been hearing about them from Jasmine all afternoon." Slight exaggeration, she only mentioned them that once.

"Sorry! I just thought you might be curious."

"Well, I'm not. I don't want to know anything about them." A fib, but I didn't want to talk about it. "Why are you always on about it, anyway?"

She looked surprised. "I'm not. But you can't very well ignore it all, can you? It's all happening."

I clutched my gigantic swollen belly and said sarcastically, "Thanks for reminding me. It might have slipped my mind." I didn't mean to be nasty, it just came out.

Anyway, I was bored and uncomfortable and fed up, and suddenly didn't want to be around people at all, not even Becs. So when she asked if I wanted to go to hers and watch a DVD or something I said, rather shortly, "No thanks. I've got stuff to do."

Like going up to my room, heaving myself onto the bed and having a good old cry.

Twenty-seven

Results

REBECCA

Poor Jade. She was not having a good time at all. She'd really been suffering these last few weeks, and I thought she was quite depressed. It really made Adam and I think hard about our own relationship. Since we'd both taken that step out on to the bridge of faith and become Christians, talking about it seemed a lot easier. I used to think that it was only a matter of time before we got involved physically. It was what everyone did – or that's what I suspected. A lot of the people I knew thought it was OK even to have one-night stands, and to the ones in steady relationships it was perfectly normal to be having sex. And since that evening in the vicarage, we knew just how easy it would have been to go with our feelings, there and then.

We'd been giving it all a lot more thought since then. We were learning, through teaching and Bible study, that God sets great importance on the marriage relationship, and that sex is a wonderful gift, but that it is precious and best saved for the person you're going to commit to for the rest of your life. Far too precious to be cheapened by casual encounters or even steady relationships that might not last. Not that God won't forgive you if you've had relationships – he will. But the best and most fulfilling thing is to save sex for marriage.

Adam and I knew we were a bit young to be thinking of marriage yet, although I did think about it sometimes. Maybe we would. But there was a lot to be done before then – college or uni, getting qualifications, deciding on careers. Maybe we'd grow apart; some people did when they went away and met lots of other people. The thought brought me out in goosebumps though. I hoped, hoped, hoped it wouldn't happen. But we'd made up our minds to stick to our decision to keep our relationship within limits. Hard, but not impossible.

I was so glad Mary and the vicar, and my parents too, didn't lecture us and make lots of rules and interfere. They trusted us, and that was another reason to prove we could be trusted not to mess up. All sounds very goody-goody and as though we could never make mistakes. Things could easily go wrong. But we'd decided to do our best, and we'd avoid those situations where things might get out of hand.

I hadn't been seeing Jade quite as much as usual, and was beginning to feel a bit guilty about it. The summer holidays had just seemed to fly by. Exam results had been good all round; Adam and I both got good grades, and considering what she'd had to put up with, Jade had done brilliantly. Not as many stars with her As as she'd have liked, but still amazing. And now it was almost time for the new term to begin.

I couldn't help thinking of Jade when I went shopping for the usual shoes, shirts, socks and stuff which meant the beginning of a new school year. Our last, in fact. I hadn't asked her to go too; with only a couple of weeks until her due date I didn't think she'd fancy trailing round the shops. But I missed her.

Mum seemed to be echoing my thought as we sat at the kitchen table sewing buttons on the new shirts. Mum has a thing about buttons, she's convinced that buttons on new garments are not securely stitched on, and have to be checked over and sewn on at home. "Do you think Jade will go back at the start of the new term?" she asked. "Or will she leave it until after the baby's born and then catch up?"

I was ashamed to admit that I didn't know. We hadn't discussed it. And even more ashamed to realise that I hoped she wouldn't go back until afterwards. Whatever would it be like lumbering round from class to class nearly nine months pregnant? What if she went into labour in school, or her waters broke or something? I'd heard that can happen without any warning. I almost went hot and cold at the very thought.

The fact was, I hadn't even seen Jade for a couple of weeks. We'd gone swimming sometimes over the summer, but she'd finally decided she couldn't face it any more.

"It's just too much bother, getting changed and all that," she'd told me the last time we'd spoken. "Everything is, if I'm honest."

She'd sounded listless and tired every time I phoned. I asked if she wanted to go for a coffee; she didn't. Actually she'd gone off coffee, but still drank shakes and smoothies. Nor did she want to come round to mine. When I'd texted her a couple of days ago, to see if she wanted me to go round to hers, I could almost visualise her shrugging her shoulders. "If you like," she had said. She didn't sound too keen, so I didn't go.

"There, that's done," said Mum, folding the shirts neatly. She gathered up her sewing things and took them to the living room. David had been lurking about by the fridge, making himself a pile of big doorstep cheese and pickle sandwiches. He brought them over to the table and sat down.

"I think you ought to go over and see Jade," he said. I looked at him in surprise. He seemed a bit embarrassed. "I mean, she's your mate, and it can't be easy for her at the moment." He was even blushing a bit, and took a huge bite out of a sandwich to cover up. I knew he'd walked home from swimming with Jade a few times, and maybe there was a bit more here than met the eye. He seemed really concerned, and I felt another twinge of guilt that I'd rather neglected Jade just lately.

"You're right," I said. "I'll go round tomorrow."

Twenty-eight

Not Right

REBECCA

I went round the next day, and the moment I saw Jade I wished I hadn't left it so long. She was just lying on the bed, looking pale and tired.

"Jade, are you OK? Have you had a check-up this week?"

"It was supposed to be today, but I phoned and told them I had flu," she said, not even bothering to sit up. "Told Susan the same. I couldn't be bothered getting dressed and dragging myself off round the clinic."

She was still in her pjs and didn't look as though she'd even put a comb through her hair. I had to admit she didn't seem well. "But won't they need to check you over?" I asked.

"It'll keep until next week, surely," she said listlessly. "I don't feel all that good, to be honest. I feel kind of shaky and I've got a massive headache."

"Oh no! Shall I get you some pain killers? Or a cup of tea?"

"Had some. They don't seem to make much difference, and I can't take any more, because of . . ." she indicated the bump. "And any more tea would make me throw up." She sighed. "If it would stop jumping around it might help." Another sigh. "I wish it was all over."

If I had a gold coin for every time I'd heard her say that in the last few months, I'd have been a rich person. I did feel sorry for her though. "Shall I paint your toenails for you?" I offered. "I've got a cool new colour in my bag, Blueberry Fizz, I think it's called."

"If you like. Can't reach them any more. Can't even see them when I'm standing up."

I wished I could do more to help. It was a comfort to remember I could pray. And I decided I must definitely keep in closer touch from now on. She really needed a friend. So I rang her the next morning to see how she was feeling, but there was no answer. *Maybe she's having a lie-in*, I thought. I tried the land line instead, but there was no answer there either, so I left a message asking her to call back. I felt reassured. It was a nice day and maybe they'd gone to the shops or something.

It was quite late in the afternoon when my phone buzzed. "Rebecca? This is Susan, just found your message." She sounded flustered. "Rebecca, I'm afraid Jade's not here. She had to go into hospital."

I caught my breath. "Is she having the baby? I thought it wasn't due for another couple of weeks at least."

"It's not due. But she might be having it. I'm afraid she's seriously ill. We called the doctor this morning. I wish we'd done it before, she wasn't well yesterday, but we thought she'd just picked up a flu bug and needed to rest . . ."

She was gabbling a bit, getting the words out in a rush. "She had this headache that didn't get any better. The doctor found her blood pressure was sky high, and rushed her straight to hospital. She has toxaemia of pregnancy. They have to get the baby delivered as quickly as possible, probably a caesarian section this evening. I've just come home to get some things . . ."

My head was reeling. I said the first thing that came into my head. "Can I go and see her?"

"No, no, I'm afraid they won't let you. She'll be in theatre or recovering – it's really quite serious."

I could tell she was in a rush to go, so I said something like hope it all goes well and hung up. Toxaemia of pregnancy? I hadn't a clue what that was, but Susan sounded desperate. I did a quick search on Google. It was not reassuring. It's so serious it can lead to convulsions, or even a stroke, and in the worst scenario, the death of the mother. Headache and high blood pressure are warning signs. Maybe if Jade had kept her last ante-natal appointment they would have picked up on it! If only I'd gone to see her more often. If only I'd got help instead of just painting her toenails!

What on earth could I do? How long does a caesarian section take? Jade could even die, and maybe even the baby, and it would be partly my fault. I felt totally helpless, and on the verge of panic. Then a surge of relief as I remembered that I could pray, and that prayer is a powerful thing. When we come to the end of what we can do, we have to depend on God, that was what Mary always said, and that was the only thing I could do now.

Twenty-nine

My Choice

JADE

That second emergency ride into hospital seemed even more fraught than the first. I didn't quite understand it, but everyone seemed to think I was seriously ill. I did feel rough, but it was just a bad headache, surely? But the ambulance crew were constantly monitoring my blood pressure and the driver was stepping on the gas, we had the siren going and we jumped at least two sets of red lights. Susan was almost wringing her hands, but I could see she didn't know what was happening, either.

At the hospital, we didn't bother with the usual A&E waiting room, I was stretchered right through the queues, although I kept saying I could walk. I had to admit I did feel very ropey, but I didn't know why I was getting the treatment. I wasn't even in labour.

I was put in a cubicle on my own, and there was more monitoring and testing and a young doctor being called in, looking as though he'd been up all night. They were asking questions and telling a nurse to put in a cannula in my hand and telling me I'd probably be having a caesarian section because they needed to get this baby out.

It was then I realised something was different. In spite of all the panic and activity, I hadn't felt the baby move at all that morning. I clutched at the bump with my free hand, and the nurse putting in the cannula looked at me and frowned. "Are you in pain, dear?"

My head still hurt but I said, "No, no, it's the baby. It's not moving, it's stopped. It's dead. It must be dead." I started to panic myself. I'd got that used to all the kicking and heaving and now there was nothing. They were trying to calm me. "Please try to relax. It may not mean anything. Babies in the womb do sleep, you know, just like us."

"Mine doesn't. Something must have happened . . ."

I could see they were worried, whether about me or the baby I didn't know. But someone put an instrument on my tummy and listened for a heartbeat, frowning a little. And there it was, hammering away, loud and clear. I went limp with relief, surprised at my own reaction. The nurse beamed. "There you go! Baby's fine."

I was not fine though, it seemed. They were scurrying about doing things, asking when I last ate or drank, checking my blood pressure, and then the doctor was back and he was looking down at me and saying, "You'll be going down to theatre shortly. Someone will be in to get you prepped very soon."

And then it all became something of a blur. They were bustling about, and Susan was being told that perhaps now might be a good time to go home and get the things I'd need, because I'd be in theatre and recovery for a while. They were putting something into my arm via a drip, and a nurse was holding my hand, and then there was nothing.

* * *

I woke and there was pain, a dull aching pain across the lower part of my body. I thought I must be in labour, but when I put my hand down to the bump, there was no bump there, only a soft mass of padding covering the place where the pain was coming from. I was still attached to a drip; a nurse was adjusting the stand. I made a sound, and she said, "Oh, you're awake." I tried to speak but my mouth was dry and I couldn't get any words out. She patted my hand and said comfortingly, "You'll be woozy from the anaesthetic for a while, but you're OK. Any headache now?"

My headache had eased, but my whole body was a mass of pain. It must be all over then. The nurse said she was just organising some pain relief, and my eyes were drooping closed and I was drifting off again, but I had this kind of longing and I wanted to cry, and I wanted my mother, and she wasn't there. Then there was nothingness again.

The next time I woke I was alone in a little room on my own, and it was daylight outside. Susan wasn't there, but I knew she'd been there, because I could see my own dressing gown draped over the back of the chair, my slippers underneath it and my wash bag on the chair seat. My mouth was so dry it felt like sandpaper, and I was still attached to the drip. There was a covered jug of water on the locker top, with a plastic tumbler. I tried to reach it but I was shaky and only succeeded in knocking the tumbler to the floor with a great clatter.

A nurse came bustling in from along the corridor, got me a clean tumbler and a drink, plumped up my pillows, and asked me how I was feeling. I wasn't sure really. I was stiff and achey, and I had a strange, empty, lonely feeling. It was all over. In a week or two, everything would be normal again.

Except it wasn't, and once again I was overwhelmed by this longing, and I wanted my mother. I didn't ever remember feeling like this before. I sobbed and sobbed.

The nurse was concerned, got tissues and made "there, there" kinds of noises. She was a different one to the last one I'd seen, and looked very young, not much older than me. She was genuinely concerned for me, I could see, and after a while she said, "I know what will cheer you up. I'm not sure whether I should do this really, but staff nurse is not around at the mo." She bustled off along the corridor. Moments later she was back, with a big smile on her face, towing behind her a clear plastic cot, and in it, a tiny sleeping baby.

My baby. I hadn't asked about it, had deliberately put it out of my mind. I'd half-thought that the adoptive parents would have been at the hospital and would have taken the baby home right away. The nurse had obviously not been told of the set up. I wanted to say, "No, no, this isn't the plan," but she was beaming at me and picking up the little bundle wrapped in a white blanket and putting it in my arms, arranging a pillow to protect my sore tummy. "Your daughter. She's beautiful, absolutely perfect, weighs almost three kilos, a good weight as she's a bit early. We didn't wake you in the night, you've been so poorly, but she's been fed and here she is. Oh, and there's a visitor to see you, too."

The visitor was Rebecca, and I saw her eyes grow round as she saw me with the baby in my arms. But

I hardly did more than glance at her, because all my attention was focused on my daughter.

She was so beautiful. Olive-tinted skin, dark hair the same as mine, long eyelashes fanned out over little round cheeks. She was in a white sleepsuit with pink rosebuds, and was making little snuffling sounds in her sleep. The nurse sounded as proud as if she'd given birth herself. "She's just perfect! C-section babies are often the prettiest, they're not so wrinkled and their faces don't get squashed and squeezed on the way out. Anyway, I'll be just outside, ring the bell if you need me."

Rebecca came close to the bed and I heard her gasp as she looked down at the two of us. I looked up at her and saw there were tears in her eyes and spilling down her cheeks. "Oh, Jade! She's so lovely . . ."

I looked at my daughter, felt the soft warm weight of her, and something was melting inside me, the hurt and the hardness that covered it, melting into something that could only be pure love. I recognised in her something I'd wanted and needed without knowing it. That something was love. The baby stirred a little and made little sucking motions with her mouth. A tiny hand with four fingers, a thumb and five perfect nails worked its way out of the blanket. I marvelled at this perfect creation in my arms. She was my child. Mine. And I loved her.

Rebecca came and sat on the bed and put her arms round the two of us. She must have been reading my mind, because she said, "Jade, I'll always be there for you. Both of you. It will be OK."

I looked up at her and knew that she meant it with all her heart. I truly had a friend in a million. I reached up and squeezed her hand and said, "I know." And then a thought popped into my mind. "She needs a name."

Becs nodded.

"I think I'll call her after my mum. Sarah. What do you think?"

We sat there for hours, the three of us, Becs and I holding Sarah in turns and just watching her, laughing and crying and talking.

I wondered what was meant to happen today. Would Jasmine come in, all efficiency, ready to hand the baby over to the adoptive parents? Would she give me a little lecture on how I'm doing the best thing for my baby in giving her up, but that I have six weeks if I want to change my mind?

I didn't need six weeks. I didn't care if there was a whole queue of suitable parents all willing to take her, because she would have an amazing life, and it would be with me. This was right for me, and she was my child; I had the right to choose.

I didn't know how I'd manage or how many difficulties and problems there might be. But she would never cry for a mother who wasn't there, like I did. She would never wonder why she hadn't been wanted; why she had to fight for herself as I had done. I would fight for her. I would be there to love her and care for her until the end of my days. She was the best thing that had ever happened to me so far, and I already loved her with a love that took my breath away.

I needed to make a new life plan.

If you have been challenged by anything you have read in this story and would like to contact the author, please send a message through the contact form on the Dernier Publishing website:

www.dernierpublishing.com/contact

If you would like to talk to someone about anything related to pregnancy, you can contact:

Instagram: **#pregnancymatters**

Facebook: **www.facebook.com/pregnancymatters**

or **www.pregnancymatters.org.uk**

More books from Dernier Publishing:

The City Kid
Clive Lewis

John Ouma has had enough of village life in the African bush. He's not interested in religion or knowing God – he wants independence, money, power and success, and dreams of making it big in the city. But life in the city has a darker side . . .

The City Kid is a gritty, fast-paced story of one young man's journey to find the meaning of life.

"I really enjoyed reading this book and give it five stars." — **Mihalis**

"The City Kid is a story of hope. Riveting." — **Patrick**

"This book was thought provoking, because this is how life really is. Reading this book has strengthened my faith." — **Samuel**

London's Gone
J.M. Evans

London has been bombed by terrorists. The government has been wiped out, there is widespread power failure, and throughout England riots have begun.

Maria saw the war planes fly over the home on the outskirts of London and watched in horror as the smoke rose from the direction of London. Now she must make a hazardous journey to London with her sister and a Christian friend they make along the way.

For Maria, the journey is also inside herself as she is forced to face issues she has never had to consider before, and discovers a side to life she did not know existed.

A gripping drama for young people.

"I just couldn't put this book down." — **Gilly**

"Very exciting, full of atmosphere." — **Eleanor**

What is a Christian?

If you have read this book, and wondered what it means to be a Christian, here's a quick explanation:

God made the heavens and the earth, and everything in it. At first everything was perfect, but sadly, people deliberately disobeyed God, and 'sin' came into the world. That's bad things like selfishness, lying, stealing and cheating. We have all done these things, and had these things done to us. We know what it's like.

Our sin separates us from God (who is perfect in every way), so we needed someone to take the punishment in our place. Justice has to be done. Sin has to be paid for.

Because he loved us so much and wanted to make a way for us to live with him, God the Father sent his Son, Jesus, into the world. Jesus was born in Bethlehem at the time of the Romans, and lived a perfect life. Jesus took on himself the punishment we deserved for our sin, when he died on a cross – he hadn't sinned like we do, but he died in our place. (It's a bit like someone paying someone else's debt for them.) Three days later, Jesus rose from the dead – he defeated death!

We don't deserve God's forgiveness, but if we are truly sorry for our sin and decide to walk in his ways instead of ours, he not only promises to forgive us, but gives us his Holy Spirit to live with us forever. So when we are a Christian, we will go on living with God in heaven, even after we die.

So a Christian is someone who:

has turned to God

has had their sins forgiven

follows Jesus (that means following his example, and making him Lord of our life)

has the Holy Spirit living in them

is looking forward to heaven!

We know all this through the Bible, which is God's word. It's great book. :-)

Would you like to be a Christian?
If you would like to become a Christian, like Rebecca and Adam, and millions of people in real life, you need to take the following steps:

Be sure it's what you want to do.
Think carefully. Do you really want to follow Jesus, and make him Lord of your life?

If you do, you need to pray. That means talk to God. You can do it anywhere, any time. (Not only did he make the whole world and everything in it, but God knows everything about us and hears us when we pray. Awesome!)

Here's a first prayer you can use if you like. (It starts 'Dear Lord' – many prayers say 'Lord' when they are talking about God, because when you are a Christian, Jesus becomes the Lord of your life, which means you do what he wants, not what you want . . . you will find out more about this as you grow as a Christian.)

Dear Lord,
I'm truly sorry for my sin. I realise now that
my sin has stopped me from knowing you
in the past, but I believe you died in my
place. I'd like to follow you from now on.
Please forgive me and send me your Holy
Spirit, so I will be with you forever.
Amen

(Amen is a word often used at the end of a prayer. It means 'let it be so'.)

Now you need to get to know God better!

Here are some steps you need to take:

1. Tell someone you have prayed. Who will you tell? Do it right now! You can contact us, too – we would love to hear from you.

2. Read the Bible. Find the book of Matthew (it's the first book of the New Testament), get yourself a bookmark, and start reading! Read a bit every day. You can read the Bible online if you haven't got a Bible yourself.

3. Carry on praying. You can pray all the time, any time, anywhere – it is the most wonderful, amazing thing to talk to God who made the whole world and everything in it! You might like to just talk about how you feel. You might like to thank him for the good things in your life. You might like to ask him to help you with things you find difficult. It's fine to make up your own prayer – you can just talk, as if you were talking to a close friend or a loving father, because from now on Jesus will be your friend and God is your Father in heaven. Or you can find some prayers online or in a book if you like. You can pray out loud or in your head because God even knows the thoughts of your heart.

4. Go to church with a friend or your family. Everyone who is a Christian needs to spend time with other Christians. If you don't know any Christians, pray the Lord will help you find some.

Remember this:

God loves you more than you can imagine!

He knows everything about you, even your thoughts.

He will always be with you – he will never abandon you or leave you alone.

If God's Holy Spirit lives in you, you have been 'born again'.

Because we are human, we will keep on getting it wrong, but every time we ask for forgiveness, we will be washed clean once again.

However you feel, trust in God. You know how on a cloudy day you can't see the sun? It's still there though! In the same way, you might not always *feel* that God is with you, but he is there just the same.

If you have any questions, please do not hesitate to contact us through the contact form on our website: **www.dernierpublishing.com/contact**

We look forward to hearing from you. :-)